Hacking Darkness

Dark Codes Book One
Marissa Farrar

D1525146

Chapter One

I slipped the wedge of cash into the back pocket of my jeans and tried to ignore the twist of guilt in my gut.

The number two hundred sat suspended in front of me, a glaring amount, taking up too much space in my vision.

The young man in the cheap suit, with whom I'd just met, gave me a final nod to say we were done. I turned from him and hurried toward the door, eager to let myself out onto the street and away from the run-down bar where we'd met. Though the place had been all but empty mid-morning, the stink of the previous night's spilled booze clung to the insides of my nostrils.

It wasn't until I stepped out onto the sidewalk and took a gulp of fresh air that I allowed myself to think about what I'd done.

Dad would have wanted you to do this, Darcy, I told myself. *He wouldn't have wanted you to struggle if you had the opportunity to do something about it.*

But despite my internal reassurances, I knew I was lying to myself. Yes, he would have wanted me to earn my own money, but he would also have wanted me to have made my inheritance last a little longer.

It wasn't as though all the money was gone. I had the house he'd left me, and despite having passed the age of eighteen a couple of years ago, I continued to allow my Aunt Sarah to live there. I no longer needed her to look after me, of course, but I didn't have the heart to throw her out. I'd put her through the wringer as a teenager—all the usual rebellious stuff—drinking, boys, sneaking out at night. I'd thrown back at her that she wasn't my real parent more times than I could count. In the end, the words had lost their sharpened edge, and Aunt Sarah had simply agreed with me. She wasn't my parent. No one was.

Most people came out of their teenage years with some kind of direction and with lessons learned. I was still floundering. The shame of what my father had done hung around my neck like an anchor I felt everyone could see. It was the reason I never got close enough to anyone to make friends, knowing it was a conversation that would eventually come around. Yet that shame hadn't stopped me today, though the weight of the anchor now dragged me down so far I felt like I just wanted to melt into the sidewalk and vanish.

I stuffed my hands into the pockets of my jeans and hurried along the streets of downtown Washington to grab a bus back to the district where my house was located. One of the buses pulled up, and I climbed on, tapping my pre-paid card to the farebox. There was nowhere to sit, so I hung from a rail and tried to keep my balance as the bus pulled away again.

Thoughts ran through my head, giving me no peace, questioning every decision.

I hadn't gone to college, though I'd graduated high school with honors. I could see my teachers' frustration when I refused to take my studies any further, my Aunt Sarah's frustration, too. I understood why—they had dreams of me being some big shining star—but after what had happened, the last thing I wanted was any limelight on me. I'd said I wanted to work, that I needed to work now I had no one else to support me. I was thrown promises of scholarships, but I didn't want them. Problem was, I couldn't make a job last either. I could never see the point, except for the money, and at first, I'd had plenty of that.

Right up until I didn't.

I reached home and let myself in through the back door. This was my house, but still, I felt like that same teenager sneaking in after a night out. The door opened onto the kitchen, which was also at the rear of the building. I headed straight to the large oak table and pulled the wedge of cash from my back pocket and dropped it onto the beaten and scarred wood. I was glad to have the money away from me. I hadn't done anything wrong, I told myself again. I'd just been resourceful. My dad would have appreciated that.

"Where did you get that kind of money from, Darcy?"

My aunt's voice from the door which led onto the hallway made me jump.

"Jesus, Aunt Sarah." I put my hand to my chest. "You scared the shit out of me. Why are you lurking around like that?"

"Where'd you get the money?" she asked again, her lips drawn into a thin line.

"That's none of your business." And it wasn't. She was living in my house, and I was an adult now. Where my money came from was none of her concern.

"It's not drugs again, is it?"

I rolled my eyes. "I smoked a little pot about half a lifetime ago. Do you really need to bring that up every time you think I'm up to no good?"

"Well, if you won't tell me the truth about anything, what am I supposed to think?"

"You don't need to think anything. I'm none of your business anymore, remember?"

Her tone hardened. "You might be an adult now, but you're still my family, Darcy, and while we're living under the same roof, what you do *is* my business."

"You know the solution to that. This is my house, and no one is forcing you to keep living here."

"Why do you have to be such an ungrateful little—"

She cut herself off before she could finish her sentence, so I filled in the words for her.

"Bitch? Cow? Tramp? You can say it. It wouldn't be anything you haven't said before."

My anger had taken hold, and already I knew I'd regret the words later, yet I seemed powerless to stop them.

But Aunt Sarah softened, and she ran a hand across her short, gray hair, shaking her head slightly and glancing away. "I'm sorry, Darcy. I just worry about you. You've never been—"

"Normal?" I supplied again

"I was going to say happy."

My heart cracked a little, and my shoulders slumped. "I don't think I know how."

"But you *were* happy," she said, "before your father died."

"Was I? I'm not sure I remember anymore."

But that was a lie. Maybe I hadn't been completely happy—I'd always had this feeling I was different, like everyone else knew a secret I wasn't let in on. The feeling was easily explained away by my missing mother, but at least when my dad had been alive, he'd made me feel, perhaps not happy, but he did at least make me feel safe.

I tugged a hand through the tangles of my blonde hair. My jeans had holes in the knees, and there was some kind of stain on the front of the long sleeved t-shirt I wore. Like everything else in my life, my appearance wasn't something I gave much thought to. "You could be pretty, if you tried," my aunt had told me more than once. But what was the point in being pretty? To get a guy? I could get a man if I wanted, regardless of whether I was seen to be pretty or not. In fact, I thought most of the men I'd dated had been perfectly happy that I wasn't some airhead who needed to check her makeup every five minutes. They'd been happy to share a can of beer, and sometimes a smoke, and know that I didn't give a shit if they bothered to call the next day.

My aunt crossed the room and slid onto one of the wooden chairs at the table. She reached out and fingered the folded wedge of notes and sighed. "It's not as though I've forgotten what day it is, Darcy."

The fight went out of me, and I sank to the chair opposite, my elbows on the table, my head in my hands.

"Shit."

I hadn't forgotten either. Of course I hadn't.

Six years had passed since the shooting. The date swept past me, to my left, and vanished behind me, as my past tended to do. My father, Michael Sullivan, had been an FBI agent. He'd been killed because of that job. No, not killed. Murdered. Murdered because of something he'd taken—a memory stick containing classified information. People claimed he'd betrayed his country by removing the memory stick from where it was supposed to have been kept under lock and key. Of course, what was actually on there was never revealed, and the memory stick had apparently vanished, though I believed the men who'd killed him had taken it. I'd been interviewed over and over again by the same agents my father had worked for, the same ones who said he'd betrayed his country, asked over and over if I knew what he'd done with the stick, or if I'd seen someone take it. But I'd been fourteen years old and I'd sat on the floor with my dad cradled in my lap as he'd bled out onto the rug we'd bought at a garage sale the previous year. I remembered the iron tang of his blood in the air, and the fear I'd seen in his eyes at the realization he was going to die. I'd never seen that before, my dad, scared. He was always the tough one. I knew nothing about the memory stick or the man who had shot him.

It had been the whole reason I'd met with the reporter earlier that day. He'd contacted me, not the other way around. It wasn't as though I'd gone looking for him. I'd let out the curse word because I knew I was going to tell Aunt Sarah the truth, and she wasn't going to be happy.

"I got the money from a reporter. He paid me to do a 'tell-all exclusive' on the anniversary of Dad's death."

Her eyebrows—mostly drawn on with a pencil—lifted. "And you agreed to it?"

I gestured at the cash on the table. "It was good money, and it wasn't as though I said anything I haven't already told people. Not really."

She leaned forward, taking me in with her serious blue eyes, a couple of shades lighter than my own. "You told the police, Darcy. Other FBI agents. You hadn't told the press." She scrubbed her hand over her face, smearing her mascara into tiny black flakes in the creases beneath her eyes. "What sort of things did he ask?"

I wrinkled my nose. "Just the usual."

"Which was?" she prompted.

I sighed and put my hand to my head, tugging at the strands of my hair in a nervous habit I'd never quite managed to break. "He wanted the personal details."

"About how he died? Surely everyone knows that?"

I shook my head and glanced down again, heat rushing to my cheeks. "About how it felt to watch your dad die when you're only fourteen. What he said to me as he lay dying in my arms." My throat closed over with a painful lump as I spoke. It had been six years, and yet it all felt so fresh.

"What did you say?"

"How it had all been a blur. That he'd been confused. Just mumbling a heap of numbers to me, over and over. Nothing enlightening. Nothing heartfelt for me to take as comfort."

My main memory from that moment had been how the same thought had repeated in my head.

Don't die, don't die, don't die, don't die ...

My aunt continued. "Did he ask about ... the other thing?"

I nodded. "Of course, but what do I know? I was a kid when it happened. Even if Dad did break the law by removing classified information, it wasn't as though he ever confided in me. Why would he have? And yes, maybe he did do something wrong, but nothing came of it, that we're aware of. The memory stick vanished, most likely taken by the same people who shot him, though there's no way of proving anything. It's not as though the killers or the memory stick were ever found."

"That we know of," she added.

I nodded. "True."

Glancing back to the wedge of notes on the kitchen table, my insides flipped with guilt again.

Had I done the right thing?

Chapter Two

The newspaper article went out a couple of days later.

I didn't want to read it. I didn't even want to think about it. Each time the thought pushed unwillingly into my mind, a horrible darkness twisted inside me, and I wished I could take it back. It didn't matter how I dressed it up or tried to justify it to myself, I'd exploited my father's murder for cash.

The money still sat, untouched, on the kitchen table, but I'd need to use some of it soon. There were bills to pay, and though Aunt Sarah contributed everything she could, she only worked part time cleaning, and it wasn't enough to run a house of this size. The possibility I'd have to sell it loomed in my future, but that was something else I was trying not to think about. While some people might want to be rid of the place where they'd watched their father die, I felt like it was my final link to him. It was the place I'd grown up. Maybe letting go of the house would also mean letting go of my childhood, and perhaps I simply wasn't ready to grow up yet, forever trapped in that fateful night when I'd lost my only parent.

Aunt Sarah had left for her cleaning job before I'd even woken up, so I sat at the kitchen table, using my tablet to half-heartedly scroll for jobs. I should go back to school and learn something worthwhile. I was smart enough, but my work-ethic was down the toilet. I struggled to see the point in anything.

The shrill ring of the doorbell made me sit up. I checked the wall clock. It wasn't even eight a.m. yet. I saw the hours in blocks running from right to left, and the total lack of structure in my day stood out sharply to me.

The doorbell rang again. Who would be visiting me this early?

Quickly, I dragged my fingers through my hair and scrubbed at any smears of mascara from beneath my eyes, trying to make myself look presentable. I'd tugged on yesterday's jeans when I'd gotten out of bed, and wore a sleeveless top, though I'd neglected my bra. It wasn't as though I'd been expecting company.

I would have to do.

The bell rang for the third time, urgency in the sound now. I hurried from the kitchen and through the hallway. Through the decorative glass panel in the front door, I saw the outline of men in suits.

My heart sank. Shit. Who was this now?

Keeping one arm folded across my bra-less breasts, I cracked open the front door and peered out.

My heart stopped in my chest. I knew these men, or at least knew one of them. Lyle Hollan had been the closest thing to a partner to my father at the agency when he'd been alive. I'd known him well as a young girl, and he'd been to our house on numerous occasions to have cookouts or watch football. I'd even received the occasional birthday and Christmas present from him as I'd been growing up. He'd been at my father's funeral, but had fallen off the radar not long after. I hadn't thought about Lyle Hollan in years, but figured him showing up on my doorstep, today of all days, wasn't going to be a good thing.

Glancing down, I spotted the newspaper I'd sold my story to a couple of days earlier held in the agent's hand.

I was in trouble.

Briefly, I debated slamming the door shut again and making a run for the back. I didn't want to talk to these men, especially as I knew what it would be about. Lyle Hollan would warn me off speaking to the press. He would berate me for telling the whole world about the moments of my father's death and say I was a terrible person to do such a thing. He'd be right, too.

I couldn't run. I had to face them, though it was the last thing I wanted to do, and so I opened the door fully.

"Hello, Darcy." Agent Hollan was a short, bulky man, with hair cut so close to his head, it was almost shorn. His light blue eyes studied me intently, lines fanning from the corners. His brow was drawn down in a frown, though I got the impression that was just his normal expression rather than him being particularly annoyed in that moment. The suit he wore stank of money, and I was reminded once more of the cash still sitting on my kitchen table, the number two hundred flashing up in front of me like a neon sign.

"Agent Hollan," I said. "I mean Mr. Hollan. Lyle."

I didn't know what I was supposed to call him.

He gave a smile that didn't quite reach his eyes then gestured to the younger, taller man beside him. "This is Agent Bayne."

From his lack of contact for the last six years, and his air of formality, I could tell this wasn't a social call. "How can I help you?"

"You had an interview published in the *Washington Express* today. Is that correct?"

My lips twisted. "I'm sorry. I wasn't thinking—"

But he lifted a hand to cut me off. "I'm afraid we're going to have to ask you to come with us."

Alarm jarred me, making me stand straighter, my heart racing. "You are? Why?"

"We can't discuss this standing on your doorstep. I really am going to insist ..."

I knew what that meant. By insisting, he was saying I'd be going with them, whether I liked it or not.

My mind tripped, trying to get my thoughts straight in my head. Surely it wasn't illegal to sell your story if it was something that happened to you? The events surrounding my father's death weren't a secret. It had been all over the papers six years ago, too, though admittedly none of the stories had come directly from me. I'd only been fourteen years old back then.

"Aunt Sarah," I said, clutching for reasons I should stay, "she won't know where I am."

"We'll have someone let her know."

"But ... I ..." I tried to think of other excuses, but none were forthcoming.

Agent Hollan frowned. "Now, Miss Sullivan, I'm afraid you really are going to have to come with us."

I glanced over my shoulder. "I need to get my purse. My phone."

"You won't be needing them."

His tone drove slivers of ice through me.

"I'm not even wearing any shoes," I pointed out.

His gaze flicked to the floor behind me, where my sneakers were lined up beside Aunt Sarah's sensible pumps and the black biker boots I liked to wear.

I didn't have much choice. With a sigh, I turned and slipped my bare feet into my shoes. I told myself it wouldn't be for long. I'd be home before I knew it, most likely with my tail even further between my legs than it already was. The keys for the house sat on the console beside the door, so I grabbed them before stepping outside, joining the two men on my porch and pulling the door shut behind me. The catch locked automatically, so I didn't need to worry about using my keys to keep the door secure. Was the back door locked? I hadn't checked it that morning. I was sure it didn't matter—I was bound to return within an hour—two, tops.

I glanced down the road to see an expensive-looking black car parked at the curb. A third man stood beside the open rear door, obviously waiting for me, his expression stern. Three guys for me? It wasn't as though I was some hardened criminal.

I started down toward where the car was parked. The other two men, Agents Hollan and Bayne, walked right behind me, one on either side, as though they were scared I'd turn and bolt. Did they think I was my father's daughter and I was going to cause them a problem?

"Look, I'm really sorry about the interview," I tried again as I reached the car. "I feel horrible about it. Honestly, I do. I promise I won't do anything like that again."

"Just get in the car, please, Miss Sullivan," Agent Hollan said.

I looked between the three men, but there was no sign they were about to change their minds. With a resigned sigh, I passed the man who'd been standing at the back door and climbed onto the rear seat. The vehicle had that new car smell, the seats a soft leather. The door slammed shut beside me, making me jump. Movement came from the outside as the men walked around the vehicle. Agent Hollan climbed into the passenger seat, while Agent Bayne slid behind the wheel. The man whose name I hadn't yet learned opened the rear door on the other side of the car then got in beside me. He pulled the door shut and sat with his back straight, looking straight ahead, not even glancing at me.

I suddenly realized I still hadn't managed to put on a bra that morning, and I wrapped both arms around myself, feeling vulnerable and suddenly on the verge of tears.

This is nothing to worry about. They'll just warn me off, and I'll be home within an hour.

I tightened my jaw and blinked hard to prevent the tears from coming. I didn't want to look like some silly little girl. I was Michael Sullivan's daughter, and he'd taught me to be strong. I wouldn't let myself down in front of men he might have worked with back in the day.

The car pulled from the curb and drove away from my neighborhood, toward the city.

The longer I spent inside the vehicle, the more anxious I became. Every muscle in my body tensed, and my neck and shoulders ached from the stress. I wanted to ask questions, anything to break this awful silence, but I didn't know what else to ask other than what had already been ignored when I'd asked it. Agent Hollan still held the newspaper in his lap, and a sadistic part of me wanted to ask him if I could borrow it for a moment. Had the reporter—Ian Rice—written something he shouldn't have? I didn't know what scruples the man had, if any. He could have made up something completely damning, for all I knew, and used his words as my own.

We pulled onto a smaller residential road to take the highway into the city.

The car suddenly swerved to a halt, and Hollan gave a shout of alarm. I sat up straighter, trying to see what was going on. A car had skidded in front of us, blocking the road. Had there been an accident? I couldn't see any signs of the other vehicle hitting anything. The door of the car blocking the road opened, and out of nowhere everyone burst into action.

"Get the girl down!" Hollan yelled.

I heard two sharp bangs, and something about the car changed, the front sloping down. The two front tires had just blown out, I realized. Then a second thing dawned on me. No, they hadn't blown out, they'd been shot out.

More shots were fired. Billows of white smoke rose from the engine of the car I was in, blocking my view of what was happening in the road ahead. Instinctively, I ducked, cowering behind the passenger seat. The agent who'd been sitting to my right leaned over me, shielding me with his body. I took a tiny amount of comfort in the fact these men seemed to be trying to protect me, though I had no idea from whom. The front doors of the car I was in both opened and the two agents stepped out to return fire, using the doors as shields.

What was going on? Who were these people?

I flinched at every gunshot.

Hands slammed against the car window beside me. I glanced up long enough to see Bayne's face pressed against the glass, his hand smearing blood down the pane, before he slid from view.

"Shit," swore the agent who'd been covering me.

He straightened, and I saw he already had his weapon pulled.

"No, don't go out there!" I cried.

But it was too late. Staying down, low across the back seat, he reached out and cracked open the door. "Stay here," he told me. He adjusted his body, kicked open the back door, then threw himself out. He was in position and returning fire before I had the chance to cry out for him not to leave me.

Movement came behind him, and I had time to let out a warning cry, but another gunshot cracked through the air. The third agent slumped forward, sliding down the inside of the car door, and ending up half on the floor behind the seat, the other half of his body on the road outside.

"Oh, God!" My hand was to my mouth, my eyes wide with fear. It wasn't my first dead body, and memories of witnessing my father's murder, not unlike what had just happened here, flashed through my head. What the hell was going on?

Someone would surely have called the cops by now. They'd be on their way. Hell, they'd be here any minute. Whoever these people were obviously hated the Feds, but that had nothing to do with me. I was just in the wrong place at the wrong time.

I debated what to do. Stay, curled up in a ball in the back seat of the car and hope no one spotted me, or open the car door and make a run for it? I hadn't seen Agent Hollan since he'd climbed out of the car. Was he still alive? Could he protect me? Indecision dragged me in every direction, certain whichever option I took would end up getting me killed.

But then the door closest to me swung open. I'd hoped for Hollan, but instead it was my worst fear—a man, tall and strongly built, carrying a gun. But that wasn't the worst thing. His face was covered in a black balaclava. Through the hole where the mouth was, I saw his lips, full, with a defined cupid's bow, and to my horror, I watched them curve in a smile.

"Hello, Darcy."

It dawned on me then. These men weren't here to exact some kind of revenge on the FBI agents.

No, they were here for me.

Chapter Three

I didn't want them to kill me, but I wasn't about to go without a fight. Trying not to think about the man they'd already shot, still lying slumped half in and out of the car, I threw myself toward that side of the car. The movement brought my feet up, and I kicked out at the man in the balaclava. I cursed myself for not having slipped on my biker boots at the door instead of the soft soled shoes.

Even so, I managed to get in a couple of good kicks, my teeth gritted, my upper lip curled. I was frightened, yes, but I was angry, too. Who were these people? What the hell did they want with me?

The man grappled at my legs, catching hold of my calves, only for me to wriggle free again. I commando crawled across the back seat, toward the body of the agent, trying to balance putting distance between me and balaclava man with continuing to kick him so he didn't get a good hold. If he did, he'd yank me out of the car, and that would be that.

I managed to deliver a swift kick to the man's face, a roar of triumph building inside me. I lunged for the open door on the other side as he staggered back, clutching his nose over the top of the mask he wore. I took satisfaction in seeing red appear between his fingers.

Freedom was only inches away. All I needed was to get through the door and run, and keep running, and not look back. I gave the agent a shove, and to my shock, he let out a groan. He wasn't dead.

"Oh, God."

I couldn't stop and save him. I needed to get help, though I felt wretched doing so. The man on the other side of the car came for me again, ignoring his bloodied nose and throwing himself through the open door after me.

I focused on climbing out over the injured agent.

A second figure, dressed in black and wearing another balaclava, stepped into view, blocking the open door.

My heart lurched. There were two of them.

I was trapped now. With no other choice, I went for the only space I had left—that of the front of the car, between the seats. Deep down, I knew it was futile, but I couldn't just give in. I prayed help would turn up, that someone would have reported the shootings and the cops were on their way. If I could survive long enough for them to make it here, I would be okay.

At least that was what I kept telling myself.

I scrambled over to the front seats, but I had nowhere to go. The second balaclava-wearing guy cracked open the passenger side door and pointed something through the gap.

I froze. A gun.

I'd known they were armed. Would they really shoot me?

"Come on, now, sugar," the second man said with a southern drawl. "I really don't wanna have to shoot you."

I stared first at the muzzle of the handgun pointed at me, and then following the length of the arm and to the man on the other end. He was shorter than the first guy, and through the holes of the balaclava he wore, I could see stormy gray eyes, framed with dark blond lashes. Was that amusement I saw sparkling behind their depths? Was the son of a bitch enjoying this?

The door behind me also opened then strong hands circled the tops of my arms and yanked me backward. I screamed and tried to wrestle away, but he was too strong, and besides, I still had a gun pointed at me. I didn't want these men to take me, but I also didn't want to end up with a bullet in my head and to be left to die on the sidewalk.

He pulled me fully out of the car and shoved me forward, my arms yanked hard behind my back, my shoulders screaming in protest.

"Thought she was gonna get the better of you," Gray-eyes said to his taller companion. I could hear the smirk in his tone.

"I like to make them sweat," the one with the busted nose replied, his voice clipped.

"Yeah? Well, she liked to make you bleed." That same amusement, perhaps even a little impressed.

"Shut the hell up."

He shoved me forward until I reached their car. My gaze flicked around, trying to assess what was going on, hoping there might be an opportunity for someone to help me, or even for me to do something to help myself. Had someone dropped a gun during the shootout? I wasn't much of a shot, but my dad had taught me when I was younger, and I'd done some practice at the range. After what had happened to my dad, I'd wanted to be able to protect myself. Not that it was doing me much good at this precise moment.

A third man, this one huge and bulked with muscle, jumped from the car. He wore a balaclava, too, and from the glimpses of skin I saw through the holes in the hood, he was black. A fourth man sat behind the wheel, seemingly ready to stamp his foot on the accelerator the moment he was given the word to go. The sleeves of his shirt were rolled up, and I spotted a multitude of tattoos running down both arms.

The big guy spoke, his voice deep and gravelly. "Man, what did she do to your nose?"

"It's nothing."

He shrugged, as though he didn't really give a shit anyway. "Turn her around."

Busted-nose, who still had hold of me, did as he was told. I struggled again, though I knew it was pointless. I didn't stand a chance against four armed men, but I wanted them to know I wasn't going to give in without a fight.

They were too strong, however, and held me still. Unable to fight physically, I opened my mouth and screamed, "Help! Someone help me!" There was no one around. Though rush hour, people smelled trouble and avoided it like the plague. No one wanted to get shot during someone else's fight. That didn't stop me from screaming, and I opened my mouth and let out another shriek for help.

The big guy leaned forward, his breath hot in my ear. "Now, now. We can't have that."

I heard the coarse rip of strong tape, and then next thing I knew, a hot hand was placed across my mouth, and with it a strip of the tape. It sealed my lips shut, and he smoothed his large palm across the tape, making sure it stuck to my skin. My words had been taken from me, and I could only make a frustrated moaning.

A sound filtered to my ears, and my heart lifted in hope. In the distance, I heard the rise and fall of a siren.

The men heard it, too.

"Hurry up," Gray-eyes said, still holding the gun.

The big guy with the muscles swiftly used the tape to bind my hands behind my back, and then ducked lower to tape my feet together. As he was bent, I wanted to kick again, catch him in the face for my own satisfaction, but I was horribly aware of the gun still pointed at me. I didn't want to give Gray-eyes the opportunity to shoot me.

The sound of sirens grew louder. *I should have kicked him,* I berated myself. It would have slowed him down, even if I had run the risk of being shot.

Busted-nose shoved me into the back of the car, and then slid in beside me. Gray-eyes ran around the vehicle and got in the other side, so I was sandwiched between them. Tattoos hadn't budged from behind the wheel, and Muscles climbed into the passenger seat.

"We've got to get out of here," he said in his deep voice. "Cops are on their way."

Tattoos didn't need any more encouragement. His foot slammed on the accelerator, and the tires screeched as he did a U-turn and sped away from the scene.

It occurred to me that I hadn't seen Agent Hollan's body. What had they done with him? Had he fallen at the back of the car, so I hadn't spotted him?

With my feet taped, my hands behind my back, and tape across my mouth, there was nothing I could do. I felt sick with fear, but knew throwing up would mean I'd choke on my own vomit. The body heat of the two men on either side of me seeped into my arms and legs. I pulled myself in, as best I could, trying to make myself smaller so I didn't have to touch them. Who the hell were they, and what did they want with me? I didn't have any money, if this was a kidnapping situation for ransom. Poor Aunt Sarah. Would they be contacting her and demanding money from her? She was a cleaner, for God's sake. It wasn't as though she had money either.

I wondered what she would do when she realized I was gone. Would she think something bad had happened to me, or would she assume I was out getting myself into some kind of trouble—drinking or meeting unsuitable men? It occurred to me that I *had* managed to meet unsuitable men. Four of them, to be precise.

A hysterical bubble of laughter filled my chest, and I choked it down so I didn't snort it out of my nose.

Where were the police sirens? I strained to listen, but with a sinking sensation in the center of my chest, I realized I couldn't hear them anymore. We'd left them behind.

Tears filled my eyes, and I struggled to hold them back. They spilled from the corners and ran down my cheeks, to catch in the tape at my mouth so I tasted salt.

Gray-eyes gave me a sideways glance and shook his head. "Don't cry."

I scowled at him. Why shouldn't I cry? I'd been kidnapped by four men. I figured this was definitely a crying situation.

The guy who I'd kicked in the face had rolled up the bottom half of his balaclava, and was using his shirt sleeve to dab away at the blood. Good. I was glad I'd hurt him. I'd hurt the rest of them, too, if they tried to do anything to me. I knew they were empty, pointless threats no one else could even hear, but it made me feel better to bolster myself up inside.

In the front, both men removed their balaclavas. My view of them was limited. I could see the short buzzed hair of Muscles, his broad shoulders peeping around either side of the seat, his biceps almost the size of my head. The tattooed guy driving had dark hair as well, but straight and spiked. I could see the image of what appeared to be a tiger's tail curled around the side of his neck. I was only able to see the backs of their heads, but though the side windows were blacked out, the front windshield was not, and I guessed they didn't want to make anyone who caught a glimpse of them suspicious. The men on either side of me had kept their balaclavas on, but rolled them up to stop right beneath their noses. *Nice to know they're looking after their own comfort,* I thought bitterly.

We drove out of the city. Each mile put between me and my house caused the sickening feeling of dread to solidify further in my stomach. I wanted to go home. I wanted my Aunt Sarah, and I deeply regretted all the harsh words I'd said to her. What if I never got to see her again? What if she never learned what had happened to me? Yes, we'd had our struggles over the years—she'd taken on a fourteen-year-old girl with an attitude who had just watched her father die in her arms. Of course we'd had problems, but we were family, and we were all the other person had. I hated to think of her alone and out of her mind with worry about me.

Something suddenly occurred to me. The FBI had come to see me because of the interview I'd given about my father. One of the agents had still been alive when Gray-eyes had pulled me out of the car. Maybe he would be able to tell the police what had happened, give a description of the car I was in now, perhaps even be able to tell them the license plate number. Of all the people who would be able to help, having an FBI agent see what had happened would surely work in my favor.

As long as he survived.

The thought put a damper on the little worm of hope that had started to wiggle around inside me, but it was still there. People had seen what had happened. The police would be looking for me. I just had to hang in there and not give up.

But as the car continued its journey, the four men not speaking to one another, I lost track of time and miles. The rear windows were blacked out, so I wasn't able to watch any passing scenery, though I tried to keep a look out the front windshield to get an idea of where we were going. If I had the opportunity to get to a phone or to use a computer, I needed to be able to tell people where I was, or at least give them some idea of the location. America was a big place, and it was easy enough to lose people here. I didn't want to become a lost person.

Tattooed guy finally spoke. "We're getting closer now."

My heart tightened. Closer to what?

"Here." Muscles handed something back to the men beside me. The tall one took it, and my eyes widened as what it was dawned on me.

A hood.

"Sorry, sweetheart," Gray-eyes said, "but we can't let you see where you're going."

I gave a muffled moan and thrashed between them, not wanting it over my head. But my hands and feet were bound, and there was nothing I could do to stop them. I couldn't even speak to tell them no—not that I thought they would listen to me, anyway. I wondered what else I might not be able to say no to, and a shiver wracked down my spine.

Gray-eyes scowled. "Hold her still, will you?"

Busted-nose grabbed me by the shoulders, preventing my thrashing. I shook my head, but it did no good, and the material was pulled down over my face, encasing me in darkness.

Immediately, everything changed. The sound of the car engine grew muffled and I could no longer smell the leather, but instead the musty interior of the bag. I briefly wondered if this bag had been put over the heads of any other women, and then pushed the thought away. If these men were in the habit of snatching women off the streets and hadn't been caught yet, it meant they were good at what they did. The fact they'd taken down three FBI agents wasn't looking great for me already.

I tried to force myself to keep my breath steady. It was hot inside the bag, and with my mouth covered, it felt like I might struggle to get air. I didn't want to panic, knowing it would make things worse. It was hard, though. The more I thought about everything, the more hopeless I started to feel.

With my face covered, keeping track of time was even harder to do. I had no way of distracting myself with spotting place names so I'd be able to give directions to someone should I manage to get hold of a phone and get someone to help me. Instead, I delved inward, to the point where I was almost in a dreamlike state, lost in the thoughts in my head, unsure if I was awake or asleep.

Finally, the car jolted to a halt, and I heard Tattooed Guy speak. "We're here."

Chapter Four

I jolted wide awake, sitting up straight, my heart thumping against my ribcage.

Here.

Where was here?

The car engine cut out around me. I froze waiting for the men's next move. The car door opened, and I felt the coolness of fresh air against the parts of my skin that were exposed—which wasn't much—my hands, the tops of my feet. I tried to position myself so the bottom of the bag over my head gaped open. A little fresh air filtered through to my nose and cheeks. It was a small thing, but I was grateful for it. I couldn't see anything more, however, the gap only allowing me to glimpse the rise of my breasts.

A couple of the doors slammed shut again, making me jump. I knew what was coming next, but even so, I let out a squeal when hands grabbed at my body. Strong fingers around the tops of my arms, more hands around my ankles. Struggling wouldn't do me any good, but my body reacted, bucking and flapping like a fish left on the jetty to die.

The hands lifted me, and then I was out of the car and there was only air beneath me. I wriggled and struggled, but they carried me with ease. I heard a high pitched couple of beeps—an alarm being switched off, or perhaps one being turned on? I listened hard, trying to pick up on any other clues to my location. But there was nothing. Literally nothing. I couldn't hear any of the sounds of a city—not traffic, or sirens, or people talking. In the city, there was no such thing as silence, but out here there was nothing. I couldn't even hear birdsong or the rustle of leaves on a breeze.

Where the hell had they brought me?

The men half set me down, and then I was scooped up again. I felt myself passing from the outside to the interior. A door slammed shut behind me again.

"She can walk now," came the deep voice of Muscles.

I was set back down on my feet, and then I felt tugging, and the tear of the tape that had bound my ankles together met my ears. I breathed a sigh of relief, more concerned with turning my feet in circles to ease the stiffness of my poor ankles and getting the blood back into my toes than I was about running away. Besides, I still had my mouth taped, a bag over my head, and my hands taped behind my back. I wasn't going anywhere.

Strong arms supported me, but pushed me forward at the same time. From the bottom of the bag, I caught an expensive polished floor, but I had no other clues about my location.

We paused as another door was opened, and then I was helped down a set of wooden steps.

"We can take the tape off her mouth now," Muscles said. Was he the guy in charge?

"Not sure she deserves it after what she did to my nose."

Internally, I gave a smile of triumph that I'd managed to hurt the tall one who'd first tried to grab me.

"I don't know," came the southern drawl of Gray-eyes, "I think losing the tape should be her reward."

There was a smack and a yell of annoyance, though I heard humor in their tone as well. I wasn't sure if they were serious or messing with each other. I didn't care either way. I just wanted the damned tape off my mouth.

To my relief, a hand, though I couldn't be sure who it belonged to, reached up under the hood. Fingers snagged the side of the tape, and with one fast motion, tore it from my lips.

I cried out as heat flared through my skin where the tape had been torn away. Any fine hairs must have been ripped out by the roots, and I didn't think I'd need to get an upper lip wax any time soon, if I even lived long enough to worry about such a thing.

"Please," I said, my voice croaky from emotion and lack of use, "take the bag off as well."

"Not yet, sweetheart," Gray-eyes growled. "We're gonna leave you here to have a little think for awhile first."

Confusion raced through me. "What? Think about what?"

"Come on," Muscles said, and I realized he was talking to the other men. "Let's give her some time to get comfortable."

"No, wait!"

I didn't know why I didn't want them to go. I should. I should have wanted them to get the hell away from me so I never had to see them again. But the idea of being left in this unknown place, helpless, unable to see and with my hands tied, filled me with terror.

Footsteps paced away from me, and then a door slammed shut. The small amount of light that had penetrated the bottom of the hood vanished. At the top of the stairs, a lock jammed into place. Those motherfuckers had just shut me down here in the dark.

Anger lodged like a hot stone in the center of my chest. I didn't know why I was here or what they were going to do with me, but I wasn't going to play nicely. A part of me wanted to sit on the ground and cry, but I clung to my anger, knowing it would be more productive than feeling sorry for myself. If I failed to get free, that was when I'd allow myself to cry.

The bag or hood, or whatever it was over my head wasn't tied on. If I leaned over far enough, I might be able to shake it from my head.

I bent at the waist and hung my head, as though I was drying my hair upside down, and tried to shake the bag off. But with my hands tied behind my back, my balance was unstable and I staggered forward, almost losing my balance to bring me crashing down on my own face. I might have broken Busted's nose, but I didn't want to break my own as well. Knocking myself unconscious also wasn't too high on my wish list.

Instead, I lowered myself to my knees, and tried the leaning forward trick from lower. I figured it wouldn't cause such damage if I was to fall. I shook my head, and then used my shoulders to try to push the bag from each side of my face. I shook my head again then placed my face against the ground, using the floor to scrape the material away. Inch by inch, I edged it higher, until finally I gave one final shake and the bag fell from my head.

I sat back on my heels, panting, and blinking in the dark. It took a moment for my eyes to get used to the lack of light—not that I had much anyway with the bag over my head. The only illumination was via a shaft of light under the door at the top of the stairs. My natural reaction was to want to be closer to it, to climb back up and sit with my face pressed against the door like a dog waiting for its owner to return, but I held myself back. I needed to check out the space I was in, see if there was any other way out of here, or if there was a chance they'd left something down here which I could use as a weapon.

Gradually, my eyes grew used to the dim light, and I was able to make out more of my surroundings. The floor beneath me was hard and cold, some kind of polished concrete. From what I could see, the rest of the room seemed to be a converted cellar.

My blood ran cold.

A double bed took prime position in the middle of the room. If an inanimate object could hold the promise of a threat, that was what it did. On the back wall was a second door, which I assumed led to a bathroom. Everything appeared comfortable enough, but it had obviously been converted for a reason. There were no windows, and a lock on the door.

The space had been created to keep someone in, and I assumed, for some length of time. I might not be the first, but right now, that someone was me.

What would they do with me, these men? And why had they picked me? Had I stumbled upon a sex slave gang? I'd read about it happening all the time in the papers, and online, how the sex slave trade was still very much a thing, and that girls were taken all the time and sold on. But why would they choose me? And why take on a whole team of FBI to get to me? Surely there were easier ways of taking someone.

I guessed I'd probably find out soon enough, but in the meantime I wasn't just going to sit here and wait. I needed to be ready when they came, and right now the biggest thing holding me back, other than the locked door, was that my hands were still bound. I'd managed to get the hood off, now I needed to free my wrists.

Awkwardly, not realizing before how much it helped to have hands free to get to your feet, I stood. For once, I was happy about the darkness. I didn't know if they had cameras down here, but, unless they were night vision ones, which I doubted, the bad light would hide me. I glanced around, trying to spot something I might use to help to free my hands. There wasn't much in here—the bed, the dresser, a table with a chair facing it. I went to the adjoining door and pushed it open with my shoulder. It was even darker in here, the light filtering beneath the door at the top of the stairs too far away to reach. I squinted, my mind piecing together the shapes in front of me. A toilet, a sink, a free-standing shower with a screen door. No bath. None of these things would help me get my hands free.

I turned and went back into the bedroom, trying not to feel disheartened. I went to the dresser and twisted my body slightly, rubbing my elbow against the corner. It wasn't as sharp as I would have liked, unlike metal or glass, but it was the best I had.

The height of the dresser meant I had to bend at the knees so the place where the tape was wrapped around my wrists hit the sharp corner. I tried to twist at the same time, looking over my shoulder to make sure I was getting the right place. I felt the corner dig into the tape and then I moved my hands up and down, trying to create a sawing motion. My shoulders ached within seconds, and my thighs burned from squatting, but I ignored the discomfort. I didn't know how much time I had. Those men could be back here at any moment, and I didn't know what would happen to me then. From my surroundings, I assumed they planned on keeping me here for some time, but I was only guessing. They could easily move me on, and the fear of the unknown was even worse.

My breathing came hard, and though the room was cool, beads of sweat burst on my upper lip and across my temples. The salt stung my skin where they'd torn the tape from my mouth, so I wiped my face on my shoulder, hoping to get rid of some of the sweat.

It felt as though I'd been doing this forever. It wasn't going to work. The tape was too strong, the corner of the wood not sharp enough. I'd need to try something else, but, as far as I could see, I didn't have any other options.

Suddenly, something popped, and my wrists felt looser. My heart lifted in hope. I didn't think I'd been doing any good, but a piece of the tape must have given way. I still had more binding my wrists, but it had been working!

With renewed vigor spurred on by my small success, I got back to work. My muscles screamed under the pressure of the awkward angle, and I knew I'd be stiff the following day, but it didn't seem like such a big deal under the circumstances.

A second piece of tape snapped, and I was able to pull my hands farther apart. With the extra movement, I pulled and wiggled my hands and wrists, creating more space between them. The tape was tougher and clung to my skin, but finally I was able to tug the last piece away.

I was free.

Chapter Five

I allowed myself a moment to breathe then pulled my arms around to the front of my body, wiggling my fingers to get the blood back into them, and rolling my shoulders to ease my strained muscles. The relief at no longer being tied up made me want to cry, but I blinked back the tears. I was frightened that if I started, I wouldn't be able to stop.

My thoughts went to Aunt Sarah. Would she have noticed I was missing yet? Would the shootout on the street have been reported and linked to me? Would one of the agents visit her at home and tell her I'd been abducted? I wasn't even sure what time of day it was, and if she'd have even finished work yet. Aunt Sarah and I had shared a rocky relationship, but she was all I had, and I hated to think of her worrying about me.

With my aching legs, I shuffled over to sit on the edge of the bed. I let out a sigh and closed my eyes for a moment. A part of me was tempted to lie down on the softness of the mattress, place my head on the pillow, and go to sleep. At least then I wouldn't have to worry about my current situation. It was a form of running away, of burying my head in the sand, and I couldn't do that. I'd managed to free myself from the hood and tape, now I just had to figure out what to do next. Besides, I didn't like being on the bed. The possibilities of what might happen to me there made my blood run cold.

I forced myself back to my feet and made my way over to the stairs. From the light under the door, I couldn't see any shadows, so I didn't think there was anyone on the other side. I was pretty sure I'd heard them lock it, but I had to try the handle to make sure. I'd be kicking myself if I sat down here, assuming the door to be locked when it wasn't.

Poised for any creaks or groans from the wood that might give me away, I slowly crept up the staircase. I reached the top without further incident then paused once more, listening hard for any sign of anyone on the other side.

There was nothing.

I knew the movement of the door handle would also give me away, but I didn't have any choice on that matter. I'd have to twist it to see if it was locked.

I reached out and then paused. I could hear voices, male and low. They didn't sound as though they were getting any closer, and in my head I pictured the men sitting in a room a little distance away. I listened hard, trying to make out what they were saying, hoping to get a clue about my location or even what they wanted with me. I picked up on fragments of sentences, none of them making much sense.

"... can't until we ..."

A different voice. "... won't be happy if he thinks you've ..."

It faded out for a moment then someone else spoke. "She might not even know ..."

Were they talking about me? Know what?

The sound of chairs scraping across the floor made me leap to my feet. Shit. Were they coming?

Leaving the door handle untouched, I scrambled back down the stairs, my heart racing, panic filling me with adrenaline. I knew I'd be in trouble if they saw I'd removed the hood and gotten myself free from the tape. They'd tie me back up again, and the thought of it filled me with dread.

Acting quickly, I snatched the hood from where I'd left it on the floor and pulled it half over my head, enough that it was on, but still left my eyes free.

I heard the catch of the lock being opened. I was so scared, I thought I might throw up. Terror filled me, but I managed to spot where I'd dropped the torn tape and grabbed it. I dropped to the floor, sitting up against the wall, and pulled the hood fully over my face, before shoving my hands behind my back, holding the torn tape, and praying they wouldn't notice.

The door opened, flooding the room with light, which I could see from the gap in the bottom of the hood. Heavy feet hit the treads of the staircase, and I tensed, my eyes wide, my nostrils flared, anticipating what was coming next.

How many of them had come down? There were four in total, but I didn't think I'd heard that number of footfalls.

"Hey, sugar." The voice I recognized as belonging to Gray-eyes. "Whatcha doing over there?"

I clamped my mouth shut to prevent me from snapping a retort back at him. I just wanted them to leave me the hell alone.

"It's been a while," came a second voice, slightly muffled. Busted-nose guy. "Maybe she'll need a trip to the bathroom?"

"I ain't taking her."

"We could let her go on her own."

"With her hands tied?"

I froze. What would they do if they discovered I'd managed to get the tape off myself? Would they punish me for it? Beat me? Or worse?

"What would he think of that?"

I stiffened. He? Who was 'he'?

"Yeah, probably best to not do anything that might piss him off."

There was a silence as the two of them mulled on their options.

"Hey," Busted said, and I instinctively knew he was addressing me. "You okay down there?"

"Cat got your tongue?" Gray-eyes added.

"I'm fine," I muttered from beneath the hood. "I just want to go home."

"Yeah, not happening, baby-doll," Gray-eyes said. "Sorry 'bout that."

"Then leave me the hell alone." I didn't want to antagonize them, but I couldn't help the bite in my tone.

Something occurred to me. The light in the room was still bright. When they'd come down the stairs, they hadn't bothered to shut the door. Which meant it was still standing open, and these guys thought I was still tied up. I knew there were another two upstairs—at least I assumed they were, though there was a chance they'd left the property—but I had the opportunity to take them by surprise, and I had to take it.

All in one movement, I launched myself to my feet and yanked the bag off my head. I was already moving in the direction of the stairs, propelling my feet and leaning forward as though doing so would reduce the distance between myself and freedom. It was only a short distance, and yet everything seemed to slow down as I reached the stairs. The two men let out yells of surprise and annoyance. I suddenly realized I hadn't considered if they might be armed. I could end up with a bullet in my back before I managed to escape.

I reached the staircase and slammed against the wood, scrabbling to race up, half-falling to my hands and knees.

About halfway, hands wrapped around my ankles, and my feet were pulled out from under me. I slammed to the wood, the hard edges of the stairs smacking my chin, stomach, breasts, and thighs. Winding me. The hands pulled and dragged me down farther. I kicked and struggled, managed to twist my body around so I lay face up. He pulled me down the last couple of stairs, and I hit the floor hard, pain shooting through my back. He was over the top of me now, my feet released, but pinning me down with his body instead. He wore the same black balaclava he had in the car, but I could tell by his stockier frame that it was Gray-eyes who had hold of me. I punched and clawed while he tried to grab my arms to pin me down. I felt his body pressing against mine, hard and ridged with muscle. He was far stronger than I was, and bigger. I was only five-three and probably weighed one hundred and twenty pounds—not that I'd bothered to weigh myself in forever.

In a final grasp for freedom, I went for his face. But my fingers only met with the material of the hood he wore, and with nothing left to do, I yanked the balaclava from his head. Dirty blond hair fell around a squared jaw, and those stormy gray eyes blinked down at me in surprise. He was only a little older than I was, twenty-three or twenty-four, I guessed.

The removal of the balaclava seemed to have reset something in us all. I'd paused long enough for the other guy—Busted-nose—to get behind me, blocking the exit, and Gray-eyes got off me and scooted back, looking awkward, like he didn't know what to do next. He pushed a hand through his jaw length hair and gave a shrug. I scrambled up to sitting and just stayed where I was. I wasn't getting out of the door now, not with Busted-nose in the way and the element of surprise gone. Not that I'd really stood much of a chance of escaping, anyway.

Busted-nose looked between us. "Ah, shit, she's seen your face now," he said to his friend.

Gray-eyes frowned. "What does that mean?"

"You know what that means," he growled. He hooked his fingers beneath the bottom of his own mask and peeled it away from his face.

What it meant dawned on me. Panicked, I hid my eyes with my hands. "No," I cried. "I didn't see anything. Not really, I promise!"

But of course I had. He was good-looking, but not in a classic way. His eyes might have been a little too close together, his nose slightly broad where it might have been broken once before. His jaw was perhaps a fraction wide, but that was hidden by a darker blond stubble. But yes, I'd seen him. I'd looked directly into his face, and it was already imprinted on my mind.

Busted gave a bark of laughter, but it contained no humor. "The only way you didn't see his face is if you've suddenly gone blind."

"I'm really good at keeping my eyes closed," I squeaked.

"No, it's too late."

"Okay, but I only saw one of you! I haven't seen the others!" I continued to argue.

"It doesn't matter. We're a team. We take care of each other, and if you've seen one of us, you might as well see the rest. The outcome is exactly the same."

Dread coiled in my gut. I knew what that outcome would be. He didn't have to say it.

Trembling, I lowered my hands from my face.

Gray-eyes had scooted backward, but was still sitting, his hands hooked over his knees, leaning forward slightly as he regarded me. I glanced to my left and saw Busted-nose looking down at me, his head tilted to one side. He was tall, well over six feet, and blond, too, but his hair was short and swept from his wide forehead in a far more conservative style. He wore a gray shirt rolled up at the sleeves. His eyes were a bright blue, but I could see the dark smudges of purple and the swelling across the bridge of his nose from where I had kicked him. He seemed far more serious than Gray-eyes. The one who was in control.

Movement came from the top of the stairs, and I saw two figures silhouetted in the light.

The deep voice of Muscles. "What the hell is going on down there?"

"It's okay, you can come down," Busted-nose called.

When I'd been in the car, the big guy in front and the tattooed man driving hadn't been wearing balaclavas. I assumed that was because they'd been up front, without the blacked out windows, and would have been pulled over pretty quickly if the cops had seen them driving around with their faces covered. They would have obviously been up to no good. They hadn't worried about me getting a good look at their faces because I'd been in the back and they'd been facing forward, though I still would have been able to give a decent description of them, though perhaps they hadn't realized it.

"It's okay," Busted called. "She's seen our faces. You don't have to worry about the hoods."

"What? How did that happen?" It was Tattoos speaking now.

"She'd gotten herself loose," he replied. "Torn the tape off her wrists."

"Damn." Tattoos took a couple of steps down. "Isaac is going to be seriously pissed when he finds out."

I stiffened. Isaac? Which one was Isaac?

Busted-nose gave a sigh of exasperation. "And you've just told her his name, idiot."

"Ah, shit."

"I don't suppose it matters too much, anyway. If she's seen our faces, what difference does it make if she knows our names?"

"I won't tell anyone," I blurted. It was the oldest line in an abductees' handbook, wasn't it? "Just let me go, and I won't say a word, I swear."

"Sorry, princess," said Tattoos, taking the rest of the steps, and not looking in the slightest bit sorry. "Not going to happen."

I could see him clearly now. He was as dark as the other two were blond. He had hazel eyes, spiky black hair, stubble across his jaw. A cleft dimpled his chin, and his cheekbones were defined. He'd donned a leather jacket since I'd last seen him, covering the tattoos down both arms, but I could still make out the one traversing the side of his neck.

The big guy still stood in the doorway, his massive arms folded across his chest, looking down on the rest of us.

"Since you've seen our faces, and you've just been told what one of us is called, you might as well know our names," said Busted-nose. "I'm Alex, and that's Clay." He nodded to the guy on the ground, who lifted a hand in a wave. "The one with the tats is Lorcan, and the gym-bunny up there is Kingsley."

Kingsley gave him a sarcastic smile then flashed Busted-nose—no, Alex—the finger.

I didn't know what I was supposed to say. Normal manners didn't apply down here. It wasn't as though I was going to say, 'nice to meet you.'

But that I'd seen them, and now knew all their names, clutched my insides in a giant's fist.

They wouldn't be letting me go anytime soon.

They wouldn't let me go, period.

Chapter Six

I realized I was still sitting on the floor. I felt hugely self-conscious, with these four men all looking at me. For some reason, I felt more exposed now that I could see each of their faces and expressions than I had when they'd been covered by the balaclavas. Gray-eyes, who I now knew was called Clay, had gotten to his feet to join his friends.

Wanting to bring myself on the same level, I clambered up to standing as well. Automatically, they each tensed or took a step toward me.

I lifted both hands. "Relax. I'm clearly not going anywhere."

For the first time since getting here, I remembered I wasn't wearing a bra. With four men standing around me, who, I hated to say it, all happened to be young and kind of good looking, I folded my arms across my chest. None of them had laid a finger on me in any other way except for holding me hostage, of course. They hadn't done anything perverted to me, though there was still plenty of time.

I pushed the thought away. I didn't want to think like that. With the four of them, and only one of me, locked down here in this convert-ed cellar, they could do whatever the hell they wanted.

No, there were five of them. I'd heard them mention Isaac? Who was he—their ringleader? The guy in charge. I'd first thought the one in charge was the muscle-bound guy still lurking at the top of the stairs—Kingsley—but it seemed I was wrong. There was a fifth man I hadn't yet met.

I remembered how quiet it had been when they'd hauled me in from the car. Even if I'd managed to get out of the cellar and then the house, was there really any chance of there being anyone around who could help me?

"So, what are we going to do with her?" Clay asked.

Alex shook his head. "Nothing. We just keep her here, like Isaac told us."

I frowned. "Who's Isaac?"

Alex glanced at me. "You'll find out soon enough."

Lorcan pushed the sleeves up on his leather jacket, an unconscious gesture, as though he was preparing to go into a fight. His brow was drawn down, and he looked like the kind of guy who had a permanent scowl on his face. "I think we should tape her up again. She's already proven how much trouble she can cause if we just let her roam around freely."

I shook my head. "Please don't. I'll behave, I promise. I mean, how much trouble can I cause? You know I'm down here, and there are four of you and only one of me."

Alex touched his bruised nose. "You're not exactly helpless."

I shrugged. What had they expected me to do?

"Come on," I tried again, willing to do anything other than have to face having my hands and feet bound, or, even worse, the bag over my head. "You can lock the door. This place doesn't have any windows. I'm not going anywhere."

"Just leave her," called a deep voice from the top of the stairs. Kingsley. "We don't know how long Isaac is going to be. She's right. She's not going anywhere. She might as well be comfortable."

He locked me with his deep brown gaze, his full lips a straight line, his eyes narrowed slightly, and my heart stuttered. He had a way of looking at me as though he knew something I didn't, and it made me feel strange. Even so, I was thankful he'd stuck up for me and not encouraged the others to tie me up again. They seemed to listen to him. He appeared a little older than the others, later twenties, rather than early, though I would have placed both Alex and Lorcan around their mid-twenties. Clay was definitely the youngster of the group, though I was younger than all of them.

"Okay," Alex agreed. He looked to me. "We'll leave you untied for the moment, but this is your one and only chance, got it? Screw it up, and you'll find yourself with your hands and feet taped together, and that bag back over your head."

I nodded to show I understood. I would play compliant, if that was what I needed to do to get through this. But inside I was raging. I wanted to throw myself at them, to punch and claw and hit. I wanted to scream and yell, to tear around the room and slam my fists against the wall and destroy everything I came into contact with. I wanted to cry about why this was happening to me, rage at God about what I'd done to deserve this.

But I knew if I did, I'd be tied up again, so instead I lodged all of my emotions in a hard knot inside my chest, right at the base of my throat, which seemed to expand until it was all I could feel. All I could think about. If I could focus inwardly, it would prevent me from attacking one of the four men around me, and only getting myself in more trouble.

"I think we're done here," came Kingsley's deep voice.

The other men turned and left me, Lorcan heading back up the stairs first, followed by Clay, who took them two at a time, and then Alex, who gave me a final backward glance before following after his friends. Kingsley stood to one side to let each of them pass then stepped out of the way to pull the door shut. I thought he was going to do exactly that, but then he leaned out and hit a switch on the other side of the door, and a light above my head flickered to life. I glanced up in surprise. So, they weren't going to shut me in the dark again, even though I was no longer bound. I looked back to Kingsley. He gave me a slow nod before pulling the door shut. I heard the familiar click as he locked it behind him.

I'd been holding myself together the whole time they'd been down here, but now I was alone once again, I allowed my legs to give way, and I crumpled back to the floor. Trembling ran through my entire body, and I clutched my hands to my face, squeezing my eyes shut and praying to be anywhere but here. I was still no closer to learning what they even wanted with me. All I knew was that they were waiting for this mysterious Isaac to appear. From the way they spoke about him, I got the feeling he was both the one in charge, and the one to be most afraid of. If someone was going to order me killed, it would be him.

I didn't want to die, I realized. I hadn't done much in the way of living my life, so far, but I didn't want it all to end yet. Not down here. Not at the hands of a group of men who thought it was okay to steal women off the street. I wondered what I would need to do to survive this. How far would I have to go?

When the shaking had subsided a little, I used the wall to help push myself to standing.

Something occurred to me. I'd assumed Kingsley had put the lights on as a gesture of kindness, in the same way he'd convinced the others not to tie me up again, but now I wondered if he'd turned the lights on for a different reason. Cautiously, I glanced up at the walls, and into the top corners of the room. Were there cameras in here? Did they regret leaving me in the dark before, and so giving me the opportunity to work my way free of the bonds and make a run for it? I couldn't see anything, but that didn't mean they weren't there. Cameras were tiny these days and easily hidden.

I hadn't peed since first thing that morning, and my bladder was uncomfortably full. I didn't have any choice but to use the bathroom, despite my fears that I was being watched. I closed the bathroom door behind me, encasing myself in the tiny space. It felt claustrophobic, but I'd rather feel claustrophobic than be spied upon. The space smelled faintly of bleach, as though it had been cleaned in preparation for my arrival. I hated to think of those men planning for my capture, or the capture of any other young woman to be held here. How cold and ruthless did you have to be to do such a thing?

I pulled down my jeans and relieved myself quickly, my eyes taking in everything else around me. There was a toothbrush still in its clear plastic wrapper beside the sink, and toothpaste to go with it. Inside the shower stall was body wash, shampoo, conditioner, and even a disposable razor and foam. They clearly wanted me to take care of myself, even if they were planning to kill me afterward. Maybe they liked the idea of a pretty corpse.

The thought was so morbidly dark I had to stop myself from snorting with laughter. The sound would have freaked me out even more.

But the razor did make me pause. I glanced toward the door, knowing it was shut, but still wondering about cameras. Carefully, I slid open the plastic door and reached in to pick up the razor. A plastic casing housed the blade, and I wondered how easy it would be to break off. It wouldn't be much of a weapon, but it might buy me some time if I was desperate.

You are desperate. You've been kidnapped and locked in a cellar by four—possibly five—men. This is as desperate as it gets.

Even so, I left the razor for the moment. If there were cameras in the other room, being in the bathroom for too long might make the men suspicious. I'd need to do it by pretending I was taking a shower or something, and right now it was far too soon for me to be worrying about my personal hygiene. Of course, if I took a shower, it would mean getting naked, and the bathroom door didn't have a lock. I'd be naked, and if the men got suspicious about what I was doing, they'd just let themselves in. I was no shrinking violet, but the last thing I wanted was to get caught naked by four men who had kidnapped me. I had no idea what they planned on doing with me, but I'd do everything I could to avoid putting ideas in their heads.

Okay, so the razorblade idea was out for the moment, but it made me feel better knowing the option was there if I needed to take it.

You might end up here for years, a little voice spoke in my head. *You might be one of those stories you read about where a woman is kept captive for years, and is impregnated and forced to have her children in that situation, so the children grow up never knowing any different.*

The possibility that I might end up wanting to use the razorblade on myself popped into my head, and I shook it away. No, I'd kill them before I'd do anything to hurt myself.

That annoying voice spoke up again.

All of them?

Chapter Seven

Now I had the lights on in the room, I was able to do what I hadn't before, and search it from top to bottom. I had a pretty good idea there wasn't going to be any other way out of here, but that didn't stop me looking. Even a grate covering a vent or airshaft might be enough for me to squeeze through, or perhaps send a note begging for help into the outside world. I might even find the camera, if there was one.

I started in the corner beside the door to the bathroom and worked my way clockwise around the room, pulling back the few items of furniture to check behind them, not wanting to miss anything. Most likely I was wasting my time, but it wasn't as though I had a whole heap of places I needed to be.

When I'd finished searching the walls and found nothing, I started on the floors. Everything was solid, and there was no sign of any way out.

Disheartened, all the fight went out of me, and exhaustion swept over me in a wave. I wanted to rest now, but I didn't trust the bed. I couldn't lie there wondering if someone was about to unlock the door and come down to me, or if someone was watching me sleep. Instead, I grabbed all the blankets off the bed and tugged them into the little space behind the staircase. The slats of the stairs helped to shade the glare of the bare bulb hanging from the ceiling.

I created myself a little nest out of the blankets and huddled in. I watched for spiders and cobwebs, but then mentally chastised myself. A couple of eight-legged critters were the least of my worries right now.

With no other distractions—no books, or television, or internet—I was left only with my own thoughts to turn over and over. I felt sick with fear about what was going to happen to me, but, more than that, I found myself worrying about Aunt Sarah, torturing myself about how distraught she'd be. She might be a battleaxe, she'd had to be to deal with me, but I was the only family she had. She'd lost her brother at the same time I'd lost my dad, and even though we could be harsh with each other, I knew she cared.

Twisted inside my own thoughts, I drifted off ...

I WOKE TO THE CLICK of a door opening, and for a moment I had forgotten where I was. It all came tumbling back, my memories restacking like pieces of a Jenga puzzle. I sat up fast, smacking my head on the back of one of the staircase treads. My head wasn't the only thing that hurt. My lower back ached, as did my ribs. I'd hit them pretty hard when I'd been pulled back down the stairs, and lying curled up on the floor had only aggravated the injuries. There was nothing I could do about them now. I had to see what the new arrival wanted. My heart beat hard, and I tensed, my eyes wide, suddenly alert, despite having been sound asleep only moments before.

Heavy feet trod down the stairs, the wood groaning in response. Through the gaps in the staircase, I saw the man hesitate, perhaps wondering where I'd gone. If he didn't know, maybe my fears of there being cameras down here were unfounded. After all, I hadn't found anything when I'd searched the place for a way out.

With my hand pressed against the back of my head where I'd bumped it, the other against my lower back, I craned forward trying to get an idea of who was coming down. Big black boots and baggy jeans, a black t-shirt, from what I could see. It definitely wasn't Kingsley—too slight a build—and he wasn't dressed smartly enough to be Alex. So either Clay or Lorcan, unless this was the elusive Isaac, but I had the feeling he wouldn't be making an appearance just yet.

Of the two options, I hoped it was Clay. Though they were all assholes, he seemed more easygoing than Lorcan. At least he knew how to crack a smile.

The man took another couple of steps, and my heart sank. Shiny black hair, and too tall to be Clay. Damn it. I was going to have to face the moody, tattooed Lorcan and see what he wanted.

"Where the hell have you gotten to?" he growled under his breath.

I was tempted to stay hidden, but what would be the point? It wasn't as though he wouldn't find me eventually, and if I made him hunt, it was sure to make his temper worse.

Easing myself out from under the stairs, untangling my feet from the blankets as I did so, I raised a hand. "I'm here. No need to panic."

"What you doing under there?"

"It looked cozy."

He had a tray in his hands, and came down the last couple of steps to slide the tray onto the small desk. "Here, I brought you something to eat." He was gruff, and didn't much like meeting my eye.

"I'm not hungry," I said, even though I was. I hadn't had the chance to have breakfast that morning, and hours had passed since then. I assumed we were well past lunchtime already, maybe even heading toward dinner. It was impossible to tell with no natural light or clocks in the room. Plus, I had no idea how long I'd been sleeping. It probably was closer to dinner time.

My stomach gurgled audibly, my body betraying my word. Lorcan glanced over his shoulder at me and raised his thick, dark eyebrows. I wanted to tell him to fuck off, but I didn't want to get myself into any more trouble. The thought of being tied up again was enough to make me clamp my mouth shut.

"Here." He stepped away from the tray to reveal a sandwich and a juice box. "You've got to eat."

He'd taken off the leather jacket he'd been wearing earlier, so now his tattooed arms were on display. I found myself staring, trying to pick out the different images marked on his skin. An eye, a clock, a rose, a skull, all seamlessly blended together to create one image. I had no idea who his artist was, but they were good, and must have cost a fortune.

"Do I have to eat with you watching?" I asked.

He shrugged. "I have to take the tray back. Wouldn't want you to use it as a weapon."

"Did the others send you down here? How come you lucked out on the job?"

His dark eyes narrowed at me. "I offered to bring it down."

"Why?"

A slight smile came to his lips. "Because a little female company is sometimes preferable to hanging out with the guys twenty-four-seven."

Creep. I wished I hadn't asked.

My stomach gurgled again. I was tempted to throw the sandwich back at him, but I was starving, and I needed the sugar from the juice carton. I could drink water from the faucet in the bathroom, but it wasn't the same. If I refused the food, the only person I'd be punishing would be myself. Besides, I needed to stay strong, and turning into some half-starved waif wasn't going to help me.

Not looking at him, I slipped into the chair at the table. My mouth was dry from sleeping, and from the adrenaline that had been charging through my veins since all this had started, so I used the straw to pierce the little foil circle at the top of the carton and brought it to my lips and sucked hard. I could feel him watching me, and so I angled my body away. I didn't know why, but out of the guys, Lorcan was the one who most put me on edge. Maybe it was because he resembled the type of guy I'd normally date in real life. I knew his type, and they tended to be assholes. Of course, this one had helped to kidnap me and had most likely shot someone in front of me, so his asshole quota was already filled.

I finished the juice and picked up the sandwich. My first bite of what appeared to be chicken, mayonnaise, and lettuce made me realize just how starving I was, and I wolfed the rest down, barely bothering to chew or breathe. When I finished and wiped my hands on the legs of my jeans, I glanced over to see him watching me with an amused smirk on his face. The expression caused the dimple in his chin to deepen, darkened by his stubble.

"What?" I said, glaring back at him.

"Nothing. I just don't think I've ever seen someone eat so fast before."

"I was hungry. Being kidnapped will do that to a girl."

I didn't want to be anywhere near him. I got to my feet, but my body protested at the sudden movement.

My back and shoulders ached from being slammed against the stairs, and the other fighting I'd done. I winced as I eased my muscles back into shape. He frowned. "What's wrong with you? You in pain?"

"I'm fine," I snapped.

"You don't look fine. I'll see if I can get you some meds."

"I don't want to be drugged."

"Relax. It's Advil. I'm sure you've had them before."

"I'll be fine," I mumbled. I did hurt, and I'd probably ache even more the following day. I didn't want to think too far into the future, but I couldn't help it. Normally, I could see my future plans laid out in front of me, running from left to right, and circling around the back off me when I was no longer able to visualize that far ahead, everything in structure, compartmentalized boxes. But now there was nothing. This had only happened to me one other time in my life, and that had been right after my father had been murdered. I'd been unable to visualize my future then, utterly unknowing of what it held for me, and I felt that way now. My past was still the same, flowing in the opposite direction until my memories faded away and slipped behind me, but my future was a dead end.

He reached out and took the tray, then paused and stared at me. He opened his mouth, and I thought he was going to say something else, but then he closed it again. Without another word, he turned and walked back up the stairs, taking the remains of my meal with him. At the top, he shut the door behind him, and I heard the familiar click of the lock falling into place.

Loneliness swept over me, and I found myself blinking back tears. I didn't want Lorcan down here—or any of the others—for that matter, but I hated being alone. Ironically, back home, I was more than happy with my own company, normally preferring it to spending time with other people. But that had been by choice. Being locked down here, against my will and completely alone was something else entirely.

I went back to the bathroom and eyed up the disposable razor again. At the moment, it was the only hope I had, but something held me back. Was it the fear of getting caught, or was I instinctively waiting for the right moment? If I was, I didn't think it was here yet. Or perhaps I knew it might be my only option, and if I used it and failed, I'd give up completely.

I heard movement from the top of the stairs again, and stepped out of the bathroom in time to see the door opening. My stomach flipped with nerves. What now?

Alex led the way, with Kingsley close behind. Clay trotted down the stairs, too. Lorcan lurked at the rear as though he knew he'd done something wrong and was trying to delay the inevitable.

Kingsley spoke first. "Lorcan says you're hurting."

I looked between each of them. Lorcan was back to not meeting my eye, looking at something on the ground that had caught his attention instead.

"I'm fine," I muttered. "I told Lorcan I was fine."

Slowly, Kingsley shook his head. "I don't believe you. Come here."

"No."

"Walk over here, or I'll come over to you." There was a threat in Kingsley's words. I huffed air out of my nose and walked over to him, holding myself as naturally as I could, though my back spasmed, my ribs tweaked with pain, and I felt my face tense in response.

A nerve beside Kingsley's eye twitched. "You *are* in pain. Show me."

My eyes widened in alarm. "What? No!"

"You know we can make you show us if we want to," Alex said.

I glared at him, too, but what could I do? They were right, and if showing them my injuries kept them away from me—for the moment, at least—then that's what I would have to do.

With my lips pressed in a tight, thin line, I lifted the bottom of my t-shirt to show the red marks and bruises where I'd hit the stairs. They were under my breasts as well, though I was still mindful of the fact I had no bra on, and I wasn't about to give them some kind of show.

"Turn around," Kingsley said, his voice gruff.

I'd hit my lower back when I'd been flipped over at the bottom of the stairs, and it was that which gave me the most pain now. I didn't want to, but I didn't want to antagonize them to the point where they took this into their own hands and tried to see for themselves. At least if I did this myself, I felt like I had some control over my own body.

Reluctantly, I turned my back on the men, and then I reached down again and pulled my t-shirt up, exposing my lower back.

Someone sucked air in over their teeth, but I was facing away and couldn't see who. I guessed it looked bad.

"Ah, shit. Sorry, sugar," Clay said.

I glanced over my shoulder to see him. His blond hair fell around his face as he frowned, his teeth digging into his lower lip. It was insane, considering the circumstances, but he did truly look as though he was sorry. Dragging me down the stairs when I'd tried to run was the least they should be sorry for, considering they'd kidnapped me and locked me in a cellar.

"You asshole." Alex rounded on Clay. "You didn't need to hurt her like that."

Clay gestured to the stairs. "She was making a run for it. I stopped her. I didn't do it on purpose."

Why did Alex even care if Clay had hurt me? I could handle the bruises a lot more than I could handle the kidnapping. And anyway, Alex couldn't talk. He was the one who'd yanked me by my feet in the car.

I opened my mouth and said so.

Alex looked to me. "I did what was necessary. We didn't mean to hurt you, though. None of us did."

Why not? Were they supposed to be delivering me to someone who wouldn't like it if I was bruised? If this was a sex trade thing, maybe the order had been put in that they didn't like their women damaged.

I dropped my t-shirt and turned around, my arms folded across my chest, hiding my bra-less breasts. "Yeah, well, you did. And you're still hurting me by keeping me down here. What do you plan to do with me? I don't expect that's going to be in my best interest either."

Alex opened his mouth to speak again, but Kingsley stepped forward. "We can't tell you anything yet. You'll find out soon enough, though, I promise."

"Why? Because you're waiting for your boss to arrive?"

They all exchanged glances.

"He's not our boss," Lorcan said, sullen. "We all work together."

"Okay, but he's the one in charge. Why else would you be waiting for him?"

Clay shrugged. "We work as a team, baby-doll. We don't do things without each other."

"He wasn't there when you grabbed me," I pointed out.

"He had somewhere else to be. But this is important, and he wants to be here."

"Where is—"

"Enough!" Kingsley stepped forward, both hands lifted. He pointed at me. "You are not here to ask questions. We're the ones who do that. Don't make me put that tape over your mouth again."

The others fell quiet. I spotted Clay and Lorcan exchanging a glance that made me think they didn't like to upset him. I wondered if I might be able to use that to my advantage sometime.

I kept my mouth shut, and Kingsley turned and stalked up the stairs. The others followed, leaving me standing in the middle of the room, wondering what the hell had just happened. Who were these guys? Some kind of gang?

Clay was the last to leave, and he gave me a backward glance and a shrug that felt like an apology, before he pulled the door shut behind him, leaving me alone once more.

Chapter Eight

The waiting around was the worst.

The not knowing.

I wished I had something to distract myself with, but there was nothing—no music, no books, not even a pen and paper so I could write. I wondered what the men's reaction would be if I asked for something to occupy my mind. I feared for my sanity if I was left like this day after day. Was it possible to lose your mind out of sheer boredom?

Of course, it wasn't only boredom. I was frightened about what was going to happen to me, and turned over every possibility in my head. Ransom didn't seem likely, considering neither I nor my remaining family had any money. Human trafficking seemed like the next most likely option, but then I didn't understand why they showed any concern for me at all. And what did this other guy Isaac have to do with it? Was he the one who'd be selling me?

With nothing else to do, I paced the room, then went to take another drink from the faucet in the bathroom. I wasn't overly thirsty after the orange juice, but I was trying to distract myself and keep myself occupied. I left the bathroom and went to rearrange my blankets in the little nest I'd created for myself under the stairs. I felt safer curled up in there than anywhere else. Even in the bathroom, though it was a small space, I felt vulnerable. Exposed.

I'd only just settled down again when the door lock clicked open. Instead of hiding, I scrambled back to my feet to see who was coming. Could the mysterious Isaac have arrived? Though a part of me dreaded him coming, another part just wanted to get on with things and learn my fate.

But it was Kingsley, alone this time. He made his way down the stairs, not looking at me, but at the small plastic jar he held in his hands. He reached the bottom and glanced up to see me there.

He held out the container. "I brought you something."

I glanced at it, my eyes narrowed. "What is that?"

"Arnica."

I frowned. "Arnica? What's that supposed to be?"

"It's good for healing bruising. I thought it could help." He started to unscrew the lid, and I realized what he planned on doing.

I put out my hand. "It's fine. I can do it."

"No," he said. "I'll do it for you. I'll do a better job. You can't even reach half of your back."

"I said I can do it," I repeated, my tone hard.

He looked at me, fixing me with those dark brown eyes. "Don't make this hard on yourself, Darcy. I said I would do it."

I didn't know what to do. Should I argue? Should I fight him? He could do a lot worse to me than just put some ointment on my skin, and he seemed to want to help, though I couldn't figure out why.

"Okay, fine," I said, scowling, but giving in.

He nodded across the room. "Lie down on the bed. Face first."

My muscles stiffened. I didn't like the sound of that, but what choice did I have? If he wanted to, he could tie me up again, bind my hands and feet. He could do a lot worse than rub some ointment onto my skin—as long as that was all he planned on doing.

Giving in to this small thing wasn't what I wanted, but I couldn't see the point in fighting. I would be the one to come off worse.

With my body tense and trembling, I crossed the room to the bare bed. I'd yanked all the sheets and blankets off it, which I'd used to create my little nest. Now it was only a bare mattress, and I was pleased about that. It was stupid, but not having any pillows or sheets or blankets helped to remove the intimacy.

I climbed onto the bed and lay down on my stomach, before awkwardly reaching around to pull my t-shirt up, exposing my bare back and the bruises littering my skin. I pillowed my face on my folded arms, my heart fluttering in my chest like the wings of a panicked bird. The mattress dipped with Kingsley's weight, and he sat on the edge next to me. I glanced over at him as he dug his fingers into the jar, drawing out a dollop of thick white cream. I couldn't look then, turning my face down, every inch of my body tensed in anticipation.

His fingers pressed to my lower back, and I flinched at the cold of the cream. But, strangely, his touch against my skin wasn't unpleasant. He rubbed firm, slow circles, pressing enough that the muscles relaxed, but not so hard that it hurt the bruising. I wondered how his black skin looked against my white—a sharp contrast that fitted so well together, like yin and yang.

"How's that?" he asked.

"Okay," I said, my voice muffled.

He finished that area and scooped out a second dollop of ointment, then moved lower, his fingers slipping beneath the waistband of my jeans.

Automatically, I tensed.

"Relax," he said, "it's not like that."

I knew exactly what he meant—that this wasn't sexual—but it was hard for my thoughts not to head that way when I was lying on a bed, my skin exposed, and with one of the men who'd kidnapped me giving me a massage. His fingers continued to move rhythmically, pressing deep into my sore muscles. He edged lower until there was a blurred line between whether he was still touching my back or the tops of my buttocks. Though I hated it, I couldn't stop the pleasure he was giving me from spreading down, sending heat racing between my thighs. I tried not to respond, yet I found myself pushing my hips down into the bed, trying to apply pressure to the sensitive spot between my thighs that needed it the most.

Kingsley finished that area, and I tried not to acknowledge my disappointment. He moved up higher, continuing with the slow, firm circles. I didn't want to enjoy him touching me, but my body responded to his administrations, and I grew sleepy with bliss. Even when his hands slipped up, over where my bra strap would have been, I didn't tell him to stop. If anything, I wanted those clever hands to rub out the kinks in my neck and shoulders as well, make me feel human for the first time since I'd been kidnapped that morning.

The thought broke me from my reverie. This man had kidnapped me. Just because he was showing me a little kindness now didn't excuse him from that. I was still in exactly the same position.

"Roll over," Kingsley said in his deep, smooth voice. "I'll do your front."

That snapped me out of it. I rolled away from him, yanking down my t-shirt as I did so. "I can reach my front!"

He continued to watch me, unperturbed by my outburst. He shrugged and handed me the plastic jar. "Suit yourself. I was only trying to help."

I snatched the cream out of his hand. "You can help by letting me out of this damned cellar."

He shook his head. "You know I can't do that."

"Then we have nothing more to say to each other."

He nodded and got to his feet. He really was a fine build of a man, and the shirt he wore did little to hide the muscles bulging beneath the material. His touch had been so tender, considering the size of him, but I didn't doubt he had the capability for violence inside him. These men had shot the FBI agents who'd taken me from my house. I couldn't allow myself to forget that they were dangerous, even if they were all young and good looking, though Kingsley wasn't as young as the others. I didn't mind that. I felt as though he was the most steady of the four, Alex the hotheaded one, Lorcan moody, and Clay more playful. I wondered what Isaac would be like—the most dangerous one, perhaps?

Kingsley turned and left me holding the jar, the feel of his fingers still ghosting across my skin. I already missed the feel of the massage, but I couldn't encourage him. It was a crazy and risky road to travel down—not that I wasn't already heading well down that route.

I watched his broad, strong back and shoulders as he mounted the stairs, trying to stop my gaze slipping lower, to take in the sight of his very firm, rounded buttocks moving beneath his slacks, and how the muscles of his thighs strained at the pants he wore. It had been a while, admittedly, since I'd been with a guy, but I didn't think I was so desperate as to start eyeing up my kidnapper, or at least one of them. Not that the others weren't also eyeing-up material, because they certainly were, but they were also a group of kidnapping killers who wanted to do God-only-knew-what with me. Though I knew I had a twisted mind, I couldn't allow myself to think those kinds of things.

I waited until he'd left the room and locked the door behind him, before I allowed myself to fall back onto the bed, my hands covering my face. What the hell had I gotten myself into here? I was losing my mind. I couldn't get the feel of those big, strong hands all over my body out of my mind. The stirrings he'd elicited in me hadn't faded since I'd told him to stop. If anything, they'd only grown stronger, and my imagination wandered to what would have happened if I'd lain back and allowed him to continue. I knew I shouldn't be thinking this way—the man was part of a team who had kidnapped me—and yet sometimes the deepest desires stemmed from the things we were supposed to want the least.

The urge to slip my hand between my thighs and finish what he had started was overwhelming. Flutterings of arousal rose higher through my core, and I squeezed my legs together, trying to control them and only succeeding in making things worse.

Damn. I needed to snap myself out of it.

I wasn't about to take a cold shower, but some water on my face should help.

What if his hands had kept moving lower, his fingers slipping between your cheeks, brushing over your ass and dipping lower ...

I squeezed my eyes shut and shook my head, trying to dispel the image. But still my mind wondered what it would be like to be with a man of his size. He'd make me feel tiny, his body engulfing mine, his strength powerless to fight against. Would his cock be as big as the rest of him? Would he struggle to fit inside me, or would I be so wet by that point my body would be ready and willing to take him?

As my thoughts had progressed, so my hips rocked against the rim of the sink. The perfect height to put pressure on my clit. Still mindful of the cameras, I knew they wouldn't be able to tell what I was doing. My back arched over, my chin to my chest, my eyes slipping shut. *Bad, bad, bad. Wrong, wrong, wrong.* And yet it felt so good. I knew the insides of my panties would be soaked by now—they'd already grown wet from Kingsley touching me.

The muscles in the backs of my thighs and calves clenched, my toes curling against the insides of the sneakers I still wore. My movements grew faster, and with it my breathing changed, first little gasps, then trapping the air inside my lungs as I built higher and higher. God, I was so close and I hadn't even touched myself properly. My mind stayed with Kingsley, with the thought of him pushing inside me, so big and forceful.

I came hard, my core pulsing and sending rushes of pleasure through my entire body. I wished I had something inside me to clench against. The little cries I gave as I came sounded too loud in the confines of the small bathroom, and I hoped that if they did have cameras, they didn't have any sound on them.

As the final waves of my orgasm faded, I wasn't filled with the normal sense of bliss, but instead shame and humiliation swept over me. What the hell was wrong with me?

I remained panting at the sink as my heartrate dropped back to normal. Not knowing what else to do with myself, I left the scene of my crime and went back to the bed where Kingsley had given me the massage.

I lay down and rolled over onto my side and curled up in the fetal position. I didn't know the exact time, but I figured it must be heading into nighttime by now. Though I'd already had a nap, with nothing else to do and wanting to escape my current situation, if only in my head, I allowed myself to sleep.

I WAS BACK IN MY HOUSE, my father standing in front of me. I could tell by the way his brow was drawn down, his lips thinned into a line, that he was mad at me about something, but I couldn't tell what. Behind him, the patio doors led out to darkness, and I knew it was night. Deep down, a part of me knew he shouldn't be here. My father was dead, but that didn't stop the delight and hope building inside of me. Perhaps I was wrong, and he wasn't dead after all. Maybe *that* had been the dream and this was real.

He looked exactly like he had that night. He'd always been a handsome man, dark hair, just starting to salt and pepper, strong and athletic from the runs he liked to do on the weekend. He wore one of the many suits he owned, and I remembered the scent of the polish he used while shining up his shoes every Sunday night.

"Dad—" I started, wanting to tell him how good it was to see him and how much I had missed him, but he lifted a hand and cut me off.

"No, Darcy. I don't want to hear it. Every time I give you a little freedom, you betray my trust."

My heart sank. I was unable to stop the words coming out of my mouth, the exact same words I'd said on that night. "It was only ten minutes. Jeesh. Why do you have to make a big deal out of everything?"

"It's a lack of respect. I tell you a time to be home, you should stick to it. It's not as though you're someone who loses track of time, Darcy. Not with how you see things."

We'd known, even back then, when I was only a teenager, what I was able to do. Some people didn't figure it out until they were older, but my father had picked up on the differences in me at an early age. My ability at only four years old to pick out of the air exact dates of events in my short life. I hadn't just been able to count, I'd seen the numbers laid out in front of me. I was no genius. I just saw things differently than others, but because of that, I could never use the excuse of forgetting the date or losing track of time, not when I was able to see it laid out in front of me like my own mental clock and calendar.

I wanted to tell myself to shut up, that I was twenty years old now and didn't have to fight with my dad about curfews anymore, but I couldn't seem to get the words to come out of my mouth. It was as though I was on a track and was unable to deviate off course.

Because this is the night he died.

The realization caused my stomach to clench. Any moment now, shots would be fired, and then my father would collapse and die in my arms.

I wanted to tell him to get down, to move, but my mouth opened and those same words from six years ago came out instead.

"Rachel doesn't even have to be home until after eleven," I protested.

"What Rachel's parents—"

The sound of two silenced gunshots thwacking through the glass patio doors stopped my father in his tracks. Surprise caused his eyes to widen, and he glanced down at the spots of blood that had appeared on the front of his shirt. The bullets had passed straight through his body.

"Dad!" I cried, stepping forward to catch him as he slumped to the ground. I hadn't been strong enough back then, and we'd both ended up on the floor, him half on top of me. I felt something hot and wet over my hands and lifted one to see it covered in bright red blood.

The patio doors burst open, and men stepped into the house. It was them, Alex, Kingsley, Clay, and Lorcan. And a fifth, who stood in the open doorway, the night behind him, his face covered with a mask. The fifth man I hadn't yet met. Isaac.

No, but that hadn't been what happened that night, it hadn't been those men who'd come into the house. It had only been one. One who'd moved swiftly through the property, finding what he wanted and leaving again, leaving me holding my dad as he'd died in my arms. I'd thought he was going to kill me, too, but he hadn't.

I hadn't thought about my father's killer that night, but I'd thought about him many nights after. No one had ever found out who it was, and I'd been too distracted by my dying father to be able to identify him. I imagined what had gone through the bastard's head on that night. Had he given us one final glance, perhaps wondering whether to put a final bullet in my dad's head, but deciding the job was already done, and then vanishing with the thing he'd come for? The memory stick.

And as he'd lain dying in my arms, my father had babbled out apparently random numbers, knowing that I, of all people, would be able to keep them in my head.

But he hadn't considered that the screaming inside of me had blocked out everything he'd said.

Chapter Nine

I woke to find Clay already in the room. I'd fallen asleep on the bare mattress, and when I saw him standing over me, I instinctively reached for blankets to cover myself, blankets that were still under the stairs where I'd left them.

My bad dream remained with me, clinging to me like the silken threads of a spider's web, but the dream didn't matter. It hadn't been real, and the reality I'd woken to was far worse.

Clay held up both hands. "Relax, sugar. I'm only bringing you some food."

"I don't want any of your food," I said sullenly, sitting up and swinging my legs off the side of the bed. My head still felt foggy from sleep.

"Sure you do."

Scent permeated the air. Was that coffee? Bacon? My stomach rumbled, and my mouth flooded with saliva. I perked up, glancing over at the tray Clay had set down on the table while I'd still been asleep.

"Coffee's not too hot," he said apologetically. "Alex thought you might try to throw it in my face or something if we gave it to you hot enough to scald."

I shrugged. It was a fair point. That was exactly something I would have considered doing.

I got to my feet and went over to the tray. I was right—coffee, a bottle of water, a small bowl of fruit, and some bacon and toast. Whatever these men wanted to do with me, starving me didn't appear to be something I needed to worry about.

"Go on, eat," Clay said, encouraging. His stormy gray eyes looked almost hopeful, as though he wanted to please me. He dragged his hand through his jaw-length, dirty-blond locks and nodded over at the food.

I took a seat, but didn't touch anything. I glanced up at him and raised my eyebrows. "Are you just going to stand there and watch over me?"

He shrugged. "Yeah, sorry. After you getting away on me last time, I'm taking precautions."

"I'm not going anywhere."

His lips twisted. "Sorry."

I huffed out a breath of frustration. It was a good thing I wasn't one of those girls who was paranoid about eating in front of hot guys. Not that I was thinking about Clay being hot, just that I didn't give a shit about what he thought of me. An idea threaded into my mind, and I went with it.

I picked up the coffee cup and slurped it as loudly as I could, making an 'ahh' sound after I'd swallowed. Then I lifted the toast and took a huge mouthful, chewing loudly and with my mouth open. I munched and chomped, switching between the bacon and bread, throwing a bit of the chopped fruit in for good luck. The temptation to dribble a little, or perhaps spit something out, was strong, but I was actually starving and didn't want to waste good food. I glanced over to Clay to catch him watching me with his eyebrows drawn down, his nose wrinkled in disgust, and I had to choke back a laugh. Good, my little show had the desired effect. I wanted to gross him out.

When I'd finished, I sat back and let out a huge belch and then rested my hands on my distended stomach.

Clay leaned in and cautiously picked up the tray containing the plastic plates and cutlery, as though he thought I might try to take a chunk out of him, too.

"You know, there's a whole dresser over there with changes of clothes in it, if you wanted to take a shower and freshen up a little."

I shot him a glare, the good feeling from the food and my little game evaporating. "And why would I do that? To pretty myself up for someone?"

"I just thought it would make you feel better."

"You know what, I felt pretty good when I was walking around, free, like a normal person. Now it wouldn't matter how many goddamned showers I took, because you're holding me captive, and there's nothing I can do about that."

"This is for you as well!" he blurted. "It might not feel like it right now, but if we hadn't stepped in ..."

"If you hadn't stepped in, *what*?"

"Nothing. Just don't always treat us like we're the enemies."

My eyebrows practically shot off my forehead. "Seriously? You are the enemies! No one else kidnapped me."

"What would those agents have done with you?"

"Nothing! They just wanted to ask me a few questions."

He snorted and shook his head like I was an idiot. "Sure, they did."

"What aren't you telling me?"

He stared at me for a moment, and I actually thought he was about to open his mouth and tell me what the hell was going on, but then he shook his head. "You'll find out soon enough. As soon as Isaac gets here."

"When will this Isaac arrive?"

"Soon," he said. "Now, stop your yapping, or you're going to get me in trouble."

Good, I thought but didn't say. It wasn't as though I cared if he got into trouble. Hell, I wanted him to, and I'd watch and enjoy it while he did. Clay might act charming and boyish, but he'd been the one who'd yanked me back down the stairs when I'd tried to run. Though I had to admit, my bruises weren't feeling as bad today. The stuff Kingsley had rubbed into my skin had actually helped. I wondered if he was going to instigate a second performance today. I wasn't sure what I would say if he did. Would I tell him to go away, or would I throw myself down on the bed in anticipation?

No, I couldn't stop fighting and give in to them.

I watched Clay take the tray from the room then lock the door behind him.

If Isaac was on his way, I needed to be prepared. My thoughts went to the razorblade in the bathroom. Clay had suggested a shower and a change of clothes, and I had to admit that I felt grubby. But more importantly, I could use it as an excuse to try to create a weapon.

I went to the drawers where Clay had said there were clothes for me. I'd only peeked in them before, checking if there was anything handy in it for me to use. I hadn't thought I'd be here long enough to start worrying about my wardrobe, and yet here I was. I pulled open the top drawer to find underwear. A shudder ran through me at the idea of these guys shopping to buy this stuff. Had they done it with me in mind, or could I have been any girl? If so, they obviously had some idea of the kind of shape they liked their women to be, as most of this stuff was about my size. It was, however, fairly sensible clothing, and I was relieved to see nothing kinky, nothing that looked like an outfit that had been purchased to dress me up and display me in. The panties were all still in little cellophane wrappers, and a couple of tissue covered bundles revealed bras. They were a little big on the cup size, but they were better than my current option of nothing. I selected jeans—also a little too big—and a t-shirt that would fit me fine.

Clutching the clothes to my chest, I went to the bathroom. I glanced up at the corners, still unsure if there were cameras in here. Surely with the shower running, any camera lenses would steam up and the men wouldn't be able to see anything?

I used the toilet, and leaned over the sink to brush my teeth, thankful for the new toothbrush. It occurred to me that I shouldn't be thankful for anything. I had a perfectly good electric toothbrush at home. I wouldn't have needed a new one if they hadn't snatched me from the street and brought me here. I had to remember that. Even in the odd moments of kindness, or even that strange, overprotective thing they did, I had to remember that they were the bad guys.

I glanced around nervously as I rid myself of my jeans, and then pulled my t-shirt over my head. I still expected to catch sight of a blinking red light somewhere, and the idea of the four men all sitting in front of a screen, watching me undress, did something strange to my insides. I used one arm to cover my breasts, and slid open the shower door with my other hand. I twisted on the faucet, and water fell from the showerhead, hitting the base in a rhythmical thrumming that reminded me of rain.

Everything was just as I'd left it—the shampoo, conditioner, body wash, and foam and razor, all in the little silver holder on the far side of the shower wall. As I'd hoped, steam started to fill the small space, and I figured it would soon grow thick enough to hide my antics just in case I was being watched.

Moving quickly, I rolled my underwear down my thighs and stepped out of them, leaving them bunched up on the floor, and then stood beneath the water. The stream hit the areas of bruising I had, and I winced at first, but gradually relaxed as the heat helped to loosen my tense muscles. My eyes slipped shut and I leaned back, allowing the water to run through my hair, massaging my scalp and warming me through. I could almost fool myself into thinking this was all perfectly normal. I had to remember why I was there, and it wasn't to enjoy the shower.

Quickly, I used some soap to wash my body then put some through my hair and rinsed it out. I checked the plastic screen of the door. The steam had gone some way to clouding it up, and I doubted anyone would be able to see anything more than blurry skin colored movement on the other side. Even so, my heart pattered, my stomach coiling with

nerves and my mouth running dry. I picked up the disposable razor and
checked it. Could I break the plastic without injuring myself as well? I
wouldn't be able to do it with my hands. I spotted the metal base of the
shaving foam they'd provided.

Crouching, I placed the razor so the blades faced up, then lifted the
bottle of foam. I brought it down hard on the top of the razor head,
wincing at the loud crack it made. Would any of the men have heard
that?

I checked the blade. The top of the plastic casing had cracked, but
I needed more. I lifted the can up once more, already wincing in anticipation of the sound, and brought it back down. A piece of plastic hung
off one part of the blade. Careful not to cut myself, knowing one of the
men would notice and question how I had injured myself, I used my
fingers to pick it away. It wasn't enough to free the slivers of metal inside.

I used the end of the can again, being more precise, grinding and
using pressure this time instead of randomly slamming it down. I managed to get one side of the plastic away from the blade, then got to work
on the other side. The shower continued to drum down around me, and
I became aware of the time passing by. Had I been in here too long?
Would the men slam through the bathroom door at any moment and
demand to know what I was doing in here?

But thankfully, the final piece of plastic came loose and I was able
to pick the blade from the casing. I picked up all the small pieces of
shattered plastic, and held them in one hand while I cupped the blade
in the other. After switching off the shower, I opened the screen door
far enough to allow me to reach out and snag the towel. I wrapped the
towel around my body, pulling the soft material tight around the top
of my breasts, my hair wet and dripping down my back. Then I placed
the blade at the top of the towel, right at my breast bone, and rolled the
towel down one more time, folding the blade inside the fabric.

The broken pieces of the razor were cupped in my hand. I needed to figure out what to do with them. If any of the guys saw, they'd know right away what I'd done, then they'd search me and my room, and I'd lose any element of surprise.

I stepped out of the shower, and bent to pick up the clean clothes I'd brought in, using the time to scan the small space and figure out what to do with the plastic. I spotted somewhere, and quickly pretended to drop the t-shirt, giving me an excuse to bend down. I leaned forward and hid the remnants of the case behind the pipes leading to the toilet. Hopefully, the men wouldn't notice the disposable razor was missing. I hadn't seen any of them even come into the bathroom yet, so there was a chance they wouldn't think to check. Maybe they thought one woman with a tiny razor blade wouldn't be able to do the four of them much harm. They might be right, but then again, there was always the chance they weren't.

Needing somewhere to hide the blade so it would be within easy reach when I needed it, I left the bathroom and went back into the bedroom. My gaze darted around the room, trying to spot a good place. Somewhere behind the staircase, in my little cubbyhole, would be best. The area was dappled with shadows and wasn't somewhere the men could see as they were walking down the stairs, giving me enough time to grab the blade if needed.

I started toward the stairs when the door opened at the top of the stairs and Alex appeared. He saw me in just a towel and frowned slightly. I clutched the towel closer to my body, though I wasn't worried about him finding me half undressed. All of my focus was on the blade I now had wrapped up in the top of the towel. Was he here because he knew what I'd done? Had they all watched my struggles, knowing they'd come straight down here and take it off me again at the first opportunity?

"You need to get dressed," he said, his expression unreadable.

"What do you think I'm doing?"

I was worried he'd notice something was wrong. My insides felt like liquid, and it was all I could do to stop myself trembling.

His cool blue gaze traveled across my naked shoulders. The towel barely covered the tops of my thighs, especially as I'd rolled the top up to hide the blade. I didn't like feeling so exposed. I wished I'd gotten dressed in the bathroom, but it had been so steamy in there, my clothes would have been a struggle to get on, and besides, I'd wanted to figure out what to do with the blade.

Alex's gaze skimmed back down my body, alighting on my naked thighs. I watched his Adam's apple bob up and down as he swallowed hard and then glanced away. He was normally so unflustered, but the sight of my naked skin had affected him. I didn't want to go down that route, but I'd use it if I had to, and I lodged the observation away in the back of my mind for future use. If these men had weaknesses, I'd use them to my advantage. The main thing was that he didn't seem to know about the razor blade. Either there were no cameras in the bathroom, or the ploy with the steam had worked.

"Hurry up about it," he said. "You're going to have a visitor."

I tensed. "I am? Who?"

"The person we've been waiting for, and I'm sure you wouldn't like to meet him while you're half naked. He isn't someone you want to mess with."

And with that, Alex turned and left me, my hair still dripping down my back and onto the floor.

My mouth ran dry.

I was about to meet Isaac.

Chapter Ten

S till holding the towel around me, clutching the top so the razor-blade didn't fall out, I pulled on my underwear and my jeans underneath the towel, and then whipped out the blade, cupping it in my palm. I allowed the towel to drop to the floor, and quickly slipped on the bra that was slightly too big, before pulling on the long-sleeved t-shirt I'd found in the dresser.

I needed to figure out what to do with my weapon. There seemed little point in following through with my original plan and stashing it beneath the stairs, not if Isaac was already on his way. I needed to keep the blade on my person. I wanted to have easy access to it, but it was too sharp to put in the pocket of my jeans. I imagined sitting down only to have it cut through the material and slice into my skin. Plus, fiddling around to try to pull it out would cost me time, and I wanted to be ready. I didn't know what this Isaac planned to do with me, but if he saw me reaching into my pocket for something, he was bound to act first.

Thinking hard, feeling time slipping away from me, I tried to figure out what to do.

I remembered something I'd had in my jeans pocket when I'd been brought here, and shoved my hand in, feeling around for what I needed. My fingers touched the loop of elastic, and I pulled out the hair band.

To hide my actions from prying eyes, I turned and hurried back into the bathroom.

I didn't intend on using the band for my hair. Instead, I snapped the elastic around my wrist, and then slipped the blade into it, so the slip of metal lay flat against the inside of my arm. With that done, I pulled the sleeve of the t-shirt over both the band and the blade, hiding it from view.

Standing in front of the sink, I tried to push down my nerves. The steam had cleared now, running in condensation down the mirror and the walls of the shower. I lifted my hand and swiped my palm across the glass. My blonde hair was wet and tangled, matted to my head, and automatically I dragged my fingers through it, trying to free up some of the knots. Bloodshot trails ran across the whites of my eyes, and shadows the color of storm clouds hung beneath them. Though it had only been twenty-four hours or so since I'd last seen sunlight, my tan had already leached from my skin.

Isaac would be here soon. What would he want from me? What would he be like? I imagined him as the roughest and toughest of all the men, older, like a big biker or something. The others didn't seem to want to mess with him. At least I was armed now, though the blade would be useless against a gun. Still, it was *something*, and I felt less helpless by taking control, however small a thing, and not just sitting and awaiting my fate.

I left the bathroom, my knuckles pressed against my mouth. Unable to sit still, I paced the floor, every muscle tensed in anticipation of Isaac's arrival. My ears strained for any sign that he was on his way. It wasn't Isaac himself that frightened me, but the fact things would change for me when he did. I'd almost given up, thinking he wasn't coming, when the sound of heavy feet came at the door, the creaking of floorboards from the other side. My stomach crawled into my throat. I stared, wide-eyed, at the staircase, my heart racing in fear and anticipation. Was I about to learn my fate?

The door opened, and a man appeared in the doorway. The bright light of the hallway behind him caused his face to be gilded in shadows, but I could see he wore an expensive dark gray suit, with a white shirt beneath, and smart black shoes. This was not the big biker I'd been imagining. He started to make his way down the stairs, and I instinctively took a couple of steps back to put some extra space between us. I still had the blade, held by the hair band to the inside of my wrist.

He reached the bottom of the stairs and turned to face me.

Isaac was the kind of good-looking that snatched my breath and made my heart flip inside my chest. I hated that I had this kind of reaction to him. I got the impression he knew how he looked as well, and the effect it had on me, and that made things even worse. For the first time in my life, I wished I was gay. At least then I wouldn't need to worry about my thoughts being spun all over the place by the sight of a handsome face.

His light brown hair was well cut and swept away from his face with some kind of product. Designer stubble peppered his square jaw. His eyes had a spark to them, light green in color, with flecks of gold that I could see even at this distance. He wasn't overly tall, less than six feet, with a lean build which looked good beneath the cut of his suit.

One corner of his perfect lips turned up in a smile. "Now, if this isn't Darcy Sullivan."

He had an accent. Isaac was English.

I folded my arms across my chest. "And I'm going to guess you're Isaac."

He smiled disarmingly. "Your guess is correct. It's good to finally meet you."

I scowled. "I'm not going to say likewise."

His gaze flicked up and down my body, but landed back at my face. "I knew you were pretty from your photographs, but you really are quite stunning."

"Photographs?" The idea he had photographs of me creeped me out even further. Plus, I was wearing clothes that were a size too big, my face was free from makeup, and my hair was still damp and tangled. I'd never felt less stunning in my life.

"How else would we have known who was the right person to take?"

I tightened my arms around my body. "So, you're admitting that you planned to have me kidnapped?"

"Of course. You're here, aren't you? I'm sorry we couldn't do this in a more civilized way, but there simply wasn't time."

"Time for what?"

"To convince you this was the right thing to do."

A laugh burst from my throat. "Convince me? No, you certainly wouldn't have convinced me. I would never willingly have gone with you, or any of those other guys, and allowed myself to be locked up down here."

His head tilted to one side as he regarded me, his green eyes narrowing slightly. "Even if it meant saving your life."

I shook my head in disbelief. "That's bullshit. You did nothing to save my life. Your men killed FBI agents and then kidnapped me. You're totally delusional if you think anything else."

"The guys have been good to you since you've been here, though, haven't they? They were under strict instruction to make sure you were taken care of."

"They taped my hands and feet, and threw a bag over my head. That hardly sounds like I was taken care of."

"Ah, but that part was a necessity. They've already filled me in on your little escape attempt as well, so I won't blame them for any injury caused then, either."

Escape. His word made me think of the blade pressed against my skin, and my cheeks burned hot. Would he somehow read my plans on my face? I worried that the sharp edge of the blade would dig into my skin and blood would start to dribble down the inside of my wrist and run off my fingertips. I only had a small window where I could try to use it as a weapon. If I left it too long, it would be discovered.

"Where are the others now?" I asked, trying to take my mind off the razor.

He glanced toward the stairs. "Otherwise occupied. I wanted a few moments alone with you."

Fear struck my heart, and I took a step away, swallowing hard. "Why?"

"To see how receptive you'd be." He stepped toward me, and I moved back again, as though we were doing some strange dance.

Receptive? Receptive to what?

"Don't come any closer," I warned him.

He put out his hand to me, as though I was a nervous dog he was trying to coax over. "To the reason you're here. That's what I'm trying to tell you, Darcy."

I looked at his outstretched hand, the nails perfectly square, his fingers free from any sign of a wedding ring, and something in me snapped. With my right hand, I reached under the sleeve of my left, and snatched up the blade between my thumb and forefinger, pulling it from the hair band I'd used to hold it to my skin. I should have waited until he was closer, so I could have jabbed the blade into one of those beautiful emerald eyes, or slashed at his perfect throat, but I just reacted. Instead, I lashed out and caught the inside of his wrist. It was enough to make him yell in shock and pain, but the weapon slipped from my fingers and fell to the floor. I didn't pause long enough to pick it up, or see if there was a gush of blood, and instead darted for the stairs. I hoped Isaac would be more preoccupied with stopping any blood loss than he would be with chasing me. I didn't know where the other guys were, but I hadn't seen any sign of them yet.

My feet hit the wooden stairs, and I ran as fast as I could, taking them two at a time.

"Darcy!" His roar came from behind me, but I didn't let myself pause long enough to see if he was actually coming after me. I was glad I'd hurt him. Nothing like making a good first impression.

I reached the top of the stairs and burst through the door, blinking in the sudden glare of light. I had to get my bearings, but I had no idea which way was out. A hallway stretched in both directions. Left or right?

I chose right.

Where were the other men? What were they doing?

Several doors were on either side of the hallway, but I didn't want to take one for fear of running into the others. I couldn't hide—if I did, they'd find me eventually. No, I needed to get out of the house and try to get someone's attention to help me. I remembered how deserted it had sounded when they'd brought me to this place, how I hadn't heard any sound of nearby traffic. Would there even be anyone around to help? The hall reached a final door at the end, which was already standing open. It opened onto a large kitchen, windows looking out onto an expanse of gardens beyond, followed by fields, then a copse of trees in the distance. A set of double doors was on the far side. I leaned in, quickly checking the kitchen was empty, then ran over to the doors, grabbing the handles and yanking on them hard.

They didn't budge. It was locked.

"Darcy!"

Isaac's voice followed me. He'd catch me here.

Where were the damned keys? I scoured the wall, looking to see if they were hung up somewhere, then the kitchen surface nearby. Surely the keys would be here, unless the men each kept a set of keys on them. Had they been prepared for the possibility of me trying to escape?

Other shouts echoed through the house. "What's going on?"

And Clay's voice. "What the hell's happened?"

Isaac shouted again. "She's headed out the back."

"The door's locked," came the deep voice of Kingsley. "She's not getting out of the house."

In desperation, I looked around. A heavy marble pot used for grinding herbs sat on the granite worktop. I snatched up the pot, and without a second thought, threw it at the closest window. The crash and jangle of breaking glass made me flinch back, but I couldn't pause. The men would be here any second.

I threw myself at the broken window, holding both arms in front of my face to protect myself from the shards. Fresh air hit my face for the first time since yesterday, and I could smell freedom, so tantalizingly close. My forearms met with sharp glass, slicing through my clothes and skin, but I didn't even care. I just wanted to be outside, to feel the sun on my face and be able to go wherever I wanted, do whatever I wanted, again.

Chapter Eleven

H ands grabbed my waist and yanked me back through the broken window. Glass tinkled down around me, and I let out a sob of hopelessness. I'd tasted freedom, but I'd never really thought it would happen. I knew they'd catch up with me in the end.

I twisted away from the broken window to discover it was Kingsley's massive arms around me. He held onto me, perhaps afraid I'd try to make another bolt for it. Pieces of glass were everywhere, and I eyed them, a part of me still seeking freedom and wondering if I could snatch up a shard and use it as a weapon. At least I'd never taken off my sneakers, so though the top half of me might be a mess, I wouldn't cut my feet on the glass on the floor.

"Shit, she's bleeding!" Lorcan stared at me from the kitchen door, his dark eyes wide.

"What the hell are you playing at, Darcy?" Kingsley demanded, spinning me around to face him.

I looked between them all, and then to Isaac, who was clutching his own sliced wrist. He'd rid himself of his gray suit jacket, and the sleeve of his white shirt was now red with blood.

He fixed those green eyes on me, his head tilted to one side. "That didn't exactly go well, did it?"

"If you think I'm just going to let you sell me off as a sex slave without even putting up a fight, you picked on the wrong girl."

His eyes widened in surprise, and then he laughed, and to my confusion, the others joined in, though their laughter was less raucous. "You think we're going to sell you into the sex trade?"

My cheeks flamed. "Or something like that. What else am I supposed to think?"

"That there's something far more important about you than your body." One corner of his mouth curled, and he glanced down the length of me to my toes and then back up again. "Not that there's anything wrong with your body."

Alex stepped forward. "She's bleeding, too, Isaac. She might have glass stuck in her wounds. We can have this conversation later."

I shook my head. "No, I want to know."

"Alex is right," said Kingsley. "We'll get both of you fixed up, and then Isaac can explain like he'd planned."

What was Kingsley saying? That Isaac would have told me everything if I hadn't slashed him with a razorblade and made a run for it? He probably had a point, but I didn't think for a moment that whatever they were going to tell me would be something good. You didn't kidnap women and lock them up, only to reveal at a later date that they'd won the lottery and a trip to Maui for four.

But the lacerations on my arms were stinging now. I'd barely felt them when I'd pushed my way through the broken glass, adrenaline coursing through my veins. But now they were starting to smart. Blood ran down my hands and dripped off the tips of my fingers and onto the floor. Isaac didn't look much better, and I took a sick thrill from seeing his injury.

Alex beckoned me over. "Let me take a look."

I put my hands behind my back. "I'm fine."

"Don't be dumb. No, you're not. You don't want to leave glass in there and get infected. You could get sepsis."

"What do you think you are? Some kind of doctor?"

He didn't answer me, just set about looking under the kitchen sink. He emerged with a first aid kit.

"Sit over there," he said, nodding toward the kitchen table.

All the fight had gone out of me. And he was right, I didn't want to get some kind of infection. Though I would have preferred to have my injuries looked at by a professional instead of some wannabe gangster.

"Put your arms out on the table," Alex told me.

I heaved out a sigh and did as I was told, slipping into the kitchen chair opposite and placing my injured arms on the table. He picked up a pair of scissors and proceeded to cut up the sleeves of my top, first the left and then the right. I winced as the material peeled away, already sticking to my cuts as the blood dried. I had a number of lacerations, all of varying sizes, from little nicks to larger gashes, but nothing that looked life threatening. I watched Alex's face as he concentrated on my skin, his eyebrows drawn down in concentration, his lips slightly parted. It was a shame he was such an asshole. He really was quite gorgeous.

He glanced up at me and caught my eye, forcing me to pretend I wasn't looking at him. I looked around the room instead, seeing what the others were up to.

Clay was propped against the kitchen counter, one ankle crossed over the other, his arms folded across his chest as he watched us. Lorcan and Kingsley stood together near the doorway, while Isaac went to the sink to tend to the wound I had given him. I couldn't help but be distracted as he unbuttoned his ruined shirt and slipped it from his body.

My eyes widened as he exposed his skin. A massive intricate dragon was tattooed across his back, the tail dipped down into the waistband on his pants, the head resting up on his shoulder. Scales of green, gold, and red blended seamlessly together. Beneath the tattoo, Isaac's body was strong, and I could make out the muscles beneath his skin, though he wasn't bulked like Kingsley.

Lorcan wasn't the only tattooed member of the gang.

Alex spotted me looking at Isaac. His eyebrows lifted, a smile tweaked the corner of his mouth. "Distracted much?"

The burn in my face increased. "I just don't like watching glass being picked out of my own flesh."

"It's got to be done," he said, picking up the tweezers. "Now, hold still."

I gritted my teeth, my nose scrunched up as he set to work, picking pieces of glass, some so tiny they were mere specks, out of my wounds. None were so deep that they looked like they needed stitches, so that was something. I wondered how Isaac was getting on and if I'd managed to cut him deeply enough to warrant a trip to the emergency room. I figured he'd avoid it if he could. He'd have to lie about how the injury happened if he did decide to get professional help. The truth of being cut up by the woman he was holding down in the cellar probably wouldn't go over too well with the doctors.

The other men stood guard, watching Alex work on me, as though they were worried I'd make a bolt for freedom again.

At the sink, Isaac finished cleaning up his wound, and taped a gauze down onto it, before turning around to face us.

"How's she doing?" he asked Alex.

"Almost done."

And he was. He washed out the last of my cuts, adding Band Aids or gauze strips where they were needed.

Isaac watched me. "Time to go back to your room."

My stomach twisted. I didn't want to go back to where there was no natural light. "Please, I'll be good, I promise. Just let me stay up here."

"After what you just did? I don't think so."

"It was a natural reaction." I tried to plead my case. "How was I to know if you were going to hurt me or not? I had to protect myself."

"We still need to talk, Darcy, but you have to learn that you can't cut me and get away with it unpunished."

Unpunished. I didn't like the sound of that.

I turned to the others, hoping one of them would fight my corner—Alex, perhaps—but no one even looked at me.

Isaac stepped forward, looking down at me where I sat. "Here's how this is going to work, Darcy. You behave yourself, and then we'll talk.

Keep doing stupid stuff like this," he lifted his bound arm to demonstrate, "and you'll find yourself down there for far longer than necessary."

So he planned on letting me out at some point? Was that to release me, or to kill me?

I shook my head. "I won't do any more stupid stuff, I swear on my life. Just don't lock me back down there. Please."

"Come on, Isaac," said Clay. "Maybe we should give her a chance."

Kingsley stepped in. "There's nothing to say she won't try to run again. She's already proven she has it in her, twice now."

Clay turned to him and dragged his hand through his blond hair. "Maybe she won't if we explain to her the reason why she shouldn't."

Kingsley rubbed his hand over his mouth. "She'll never believe it. Not with her daddy being FBI. She'll never be able to see us as the good guys and them as the bad."

I held up my hand to get their attention. "Umm, excuse me, but I am here, you know. You can always direct some of what you're saying my way."

"I don't trust that she won't try to escape again," said Lorcan, and I shot him a glare for taking Kingsley's side. Alex, so far, had remained quiet through this whole thing, and I wondered whose side he was taking.

Clay shrugged. "She's seemed all right by me. Wouldn't we all have done what she did if we were in her situation?"

Isaac stepped in. "No, it's not time yet. She's got to learn that we're the ones who are in control in this situation. Fluttering her pretty blue eyes and looking sad isn't going to be enough to make us change our minds."

He took a couple of steps toward me, and I staggered up from the chair. The expression on his face was one I didn't want to mess with, but I couldn't go meekly. I looked to Alex for help, as he still hadn't spoken, but he pressed his lips together and gave his head a slight shake before getting to his feet. The others closed in as well, and I knew I didn't stand a chance of getting away from them. If Isaac said I was to go back down into the cellar, it looked like that was exactly where I was going.

I backed away, stumbling over my chair. I kept going, but my lower back hit the kitchen worktop, thumping against one of the big bruises I still had. I winced, but managed to clamp my pain down between clenched teeth.

Isaac stopped directly in front of me. He still hadn't put a shirt on—the bloodied one he'd been wearing bunched up at the side of the sink. Though his chest was free from tattoos, I couldn't get the image of the dragon on his back out of my mind. Did it mean something, or had he just had it done because he liked it?

"What are you going to do, Darcy? Are you going to keep fighting, or are you going to make this easy on all of us?"

Slowly, I shook my head. "Why should I make this easy on you?"

Then I darted forward, putting my full body weight behind the movement, hoping to barge past him. He grabbed my arms and pulled me up against him. My chest heaved as I felt his naked torso pressed up against my back. He wrenched me harder, pulling me in, so his mouth was against my ear.

"I see you like to do things the hard way, love. That's fine. I can work with that."

"I'm not your love," I spat back between gritted teeth.

I heard the humor in his voice. "We'll see about that."

His hands tightened around my arms, seemingly not caring about any of the cuts I'd sustained in that area—not that I could blame him. I had sliced him with a razorblade. He held me squeezed up against him, his breaths hot—excited, almost—in my ear. My pulse raced at the contact, my mind conjuring the sight of the dragon tattoo scrawled across his naked skin. A dangerous frission of excitement rose up inside me, and I caught the air in my lungs, anticipating his next move.

But, instead of anything more intimate, he pushed me forward, back out of the kitchen and into the hallway, which led to the cellar door. Isaac was surprisingly strong, and even when I tried to push back, he still managed to propel me forward.

I looked to the others for help, but none would meet my eye. Why would they? They were the ones who'd been holding me captive all this time. They weren't suddenly my allies against Isaac. They'd been waiting for him to arrive, and now here he was.

I guessed this was where the fun really got started.

We reached the cellar door. It remained open from where I'd run, and the staircase vanished into darkness.

"Misbehave," Isaac said into my ear, "and you'll find things only get worse for you. Do what we ask and they'll get better."

He gave me a little shove forward, enough to send me stumbling to the top step.

I spun around, but the door slammed shut, plunging me into darkness. It seemed my escape attempt had lost me the chance at having the light on again.

My balled fists met with the wood of the door. "But I don't know what you want!" I yelled back at him. "You still haven't told me why I'm here!"

Silence was my only reply.

Chapter Twelve

They were punishing me, that was for sure.

I was back in the dark again, the only light coming through the gap beneath the cellar door. I hunched at the top of the stairs for awhile, my arms wrapped around my knees, listening for any clues as to what the men wanted or what they were going to do with me.

The arrival of Isaac had made everything worse. He seemed cold and ruthless, and I understood why the others had been waiting for him. He was clearly the man in charge, and I didn't want to be frightened of him, but I was.

Time ticked by, and the men left me alone. I didn't know if I should be grateful or pissed. I'd been given breakfast that morning, but we were well past any meal times now. I guessed going without food was going to be another part of my punishment, together with being left down here alone. At least when the other guys had visited me, it had broken up some of the monotony. The boredom made me want to scream—I was normally never without a book, or TV show, or the internet far from hand. Hell, sometimes I'd have all three going at the same time. Now I had nothing to do, and that was as torturous as being left alone in the dark. I figured Isaac already knew that.

With my mortality suddenly staring me starkly in the face, I found I bitterly regretted so much of my life. I should have been a better person, and maybe this wouldn't be happening to me now. If I'd been nicer to my aunt, if I'd gotten a steady job and made some friends, maybe I'd be in a whole different place right now.

Memories swept over me, and I watched my past curving in front of me, from right to left. One particular regretful incident stood out to me, and with it came the sickening twist of guilt in my stomach.

I'd ruined my own father's funeral. I'd interrupted the priest giving his eulogy at the graveside, when he'd been talking about the richness of life and how it should be judged for the content, not the length. I'd lost it and screamed at the priest that it was bullshit, and how long you lived did matter.

I remembered seeing the look of dismay on Aunt Sarah's face, how she'd tried to grab for me, to restrain me, perhaps, or try to comfort me. But I'd yanked away from her and continued to scream, bashing at my head with my hands. I must have looked crazy. I knew I'd felt crazy in that moment. A handful of my dad's old colleagues were there. The ones decent enough to show up, even though he'd died in disgrace. I'd seen how they'd looked at me as well, distaste mixed with pity. I didn't care in that moment, but their expressions had haunted me since.

I'd run back to the house, where the wake would be taking place, and stolen a bottle of vodka. I'd shut myself in my room and drank neat from the neck of the bottle, swigs that burned my throat, but felt good. I didn't think it had taken more than a few mouthfuls before I was good and drunk, and the booze combined with my emotional exhaustion had the result of me passing out on the bed.

Aunt Sarah woke me a few hours later to tell me everyone had been and gone already. I'd missed the whole thing.

The memory caused my stomach to churn, turning inside of me like a bad meal. I wished I could go back and change things. Be responsible. Make my dad proud. But fourteen-year-old me and twenty-year-old me were miles apart, and such a thing was impossible.

I had to live with what I'd done, though for all I knew, it wouldn't be for much longer.

A horrifying thought came to me. What if something happened to the men, and no one else knew I was down here? If I couldn't get the door open, I would starve to death. I had water from the bathroom, but there was nothing to eat. It would be a long, painful death, and the thought of it scared me far more than the anger of any of the five men did.

With my heart racing, I ran back up the stairs and pounded my fists against the door.

"Hey! You've got to let me out! Please! I haven't done anything wrong. You might even have the wrong girl, for all you know. Come on, just let me out. I'll be good, I promise."

Unbidden tears sprang from my eyes and spilled down my cheeks. I wasn't a big crier, and I hated feeling sorry for myself, but I couldn't help it. I hated feeling so helpless.

"Alex," I pleaded. "Kingsley? Clay? Are you out there? Can you hear me? I've been good, haven't I? Isaac scared me. I'm sorry about what I did. Come on, guys. Please!"

I paused again, listening. My hitching breath was the only thing that broke up the silence. Could they hear me? Were they all sitting around a table, looking at each other and wondering what to do, feeling bad for keeping me here and hearing me cry? Or did they not give a shit? Were they in another part of the property, drinking beer and laughing it up, not caring about the woman they had locked in the basement?

Why did that hurt me more than the idea of them sitting around a table feeling bad about what they'd done to me? Was I harboring some pathetic idea that these men—well, maybe not Isaac, but the others—actually gave a crap about what happened to me? Just because they'd shown me a few moments of kindness didn't mean they cared.

I'd read about this somewhere. Wasn't it a type of syndrome, where the captive fell for the captor? The name came to me. Stockholm syndrome. It was some kind of survival mechanism where the person who'd been taken captive aligned themselves with the captor in order to get through the experience. But that wasn't me, surely? It had only been a couple of days now, and I was too smart to fall for something like that, wasn't I?

No, I wouldn't let it be me. These men were the enemies, no matter what.

I took my anger and wiped away my tears.

"Hey! You'll pay for this, you sons of bitches! I'll kill every last one of you, if I get the chance. You think getting cut was bad? Next time it will be your throat. You hear me, Isaac?" I pounded my fists against the door, hard enough to hurt. My hands would be red and bruised the next day. "You hear me, you sick son of a bitch? You won't get away with this!"

I screamed at the shut door in rage and frustration, shrieked until my throat hurt. Desperate for a release for my anger, I ran down the stairs, jumping the final few, and ran into the bathroom. Breathing hard in the dark, I felt around and picked up the bottles of shampoo and body wash and hurled them at the wall, kicking out at them when they bounced off and slid near me again. I ripped the toilet roll off the wall and shredded the paper with my clawed fingers, so tiny pieces floated down around me like snow. Leaving the bathroom, I felt my way to the dresser and yanked out the drawers as far as they would come then grabbed handfuls of clothing and threw them to the floor. With another yell of frustration, I tried to push over the dresser, but it was too heavy, and all I could do was beat my fists against it. All I wanted was destruction, to make the tiny, confined world around me reflect what was going on inside both my head and heart.

Had they hoped to break me by keeping me locked up, thinking I would turn into some compliant wreck willing to do whatever they wanted? Because I wouldn't do that. They'd picked the wrong girl.

Panting and exhausted, I slumped onto the floor and put my head in my hands. They weren't listening. They didn't care how much noise I made. There was no one around for miles, though I had no idea where we were. We'd driven for hours to get here, and I hadn't heard any sounds of traffic. We could literally be in the middle of nowhere.

All I could do was what they'd told me to—behave myself and wait for whatever plan they had for me next.

Chapter Thirteen

Eventually, I gave up and fell asleep, curled up under the stairs, wrapped in the sheets from the bed.

When I woke from a sleep that was plagued with nightmares, my whole body hurt. The stinging from the cuts on my arms had dulled to a throb, and the bruising only hurt if I pressed on it. But my muscles ached as though I'd done a ten-mile run, and no amount of stretching seemed to loosen the knots. My escape attempt had been harder on my body than I'd thought, and I figured sleeping on the cold floor rather than the bed wouldn't have helped things either.

My mind went to home, wishing desperately that I was in my own bedroom.

Would Aunt Sarah be losing hope by now? How many hours was it supposed to be that were the most crucial in finding a missing person. Twenty-four? Forty-eight? I didn't know, but I was sure my time down here was well past it now. This was my third day, and I could visualize my previous days held captive. Strangely, they were in a different time-line than the rest of my past, as though being taken had reset things. I could no longer see my future. My vision of it stopped on the here and now, the moment I currently existed in. Unlike others who viewed things the way I did, I'd never been someone who was meticulously organized and into planning, but I'd always had structure—birthdays, holidays, job interviews, and even school events, when I'd taken part in such a thing. Now there was nothing.

Would Isaac come down to me today? Or would he leave me to stew for longer, perhaps hoping to break my spirit? I wished he'd never come here, and I'd been left with the four other guys. I felt sure I would have been able to work my way around them, but Isaac put things into a whole new category. No wonder the others had all been told to wait until he'd arrived before speaking to me.

I untangled myself from the sheets and went to the bathroom, patting my way around in the dark so I didn't trip over anything I'd thrown around during my freak-out the previous evening. I stuck my mouth under the faucet and turned it on, gulping down the cool water. I was dehydrated from yesterday, my throat sore from screaming, and my mouth dry from all the adrenaline that had been surging around my body. The water sloshed uneasily in my stomach. It was the only thing in there, my meal of bacon, toast, and fruit from yesterday long digested. I took a couple of deep breaths, not wanting to throw the water back up again.

The click of the door made me freeze, and I glanced over my shoulder. The light in the room had changed. Someone had opened the door.

My heart beat harder, and I squeezed my fists together to contain my emotions. As much as I wanted to throw myself at Isaac and claw his eyes out, it was smarter to stay calm. I didn't want to die down in this hole, and I felt sure that was what would happen if I didn't keep my shit together.

I turned around and poked my head out of the bathroom door and looked in the direction of the stairs.

My stomach sank.

Isaac stood at the bottom of the stairs wearing a suit identical to the one he'd been wearing the day before. The one I'd ruined. He was also alone. I wished one of the other men was with him.

He spotted me peeping out at him and offered me a slow nod.

"Hello again, Darcy. I hope we can start on a better foot today."

I didn't reply, and instead pressed my lips together, my nostrils flaring. I was worried what would come out of my mouth would only get me in more trouble. But I stepped out of the bathroom, coming to face him. I didn't want him to think I was hiding away.

"You've been on my mind all night," he continued, taking a few paces toward me, his eyes glued to my face. "It bothers me how this has all turned out. I knew it wasn't going to be easy, and there would be some blurred lines about what was right and wrong, but I'd never intended for you to get hurt."

"Well, I did," I snapped.

His mouth tightened, and he gave an almost imperceptible nod. "Yes, you've been hurt, but none of us has hurt you. I hope you can see that."

My jaw dropped. "You kidnapped me!"

He held my gaze, unflinching. "That was done to protect you."

"Protect me? From who?"

"The same men who killed Michael Sullivan—your father."

I felt as though he had punched me in the gut. My breath expelled from my lungs, and I pressed my hand to my chest as though I could prevent my emotions from bursting from my ribcage. "What the hell are you talking about?"

He gestured into the air between us, his fingers spread wide to highlight his point. "Try to stop thinking of us as the bad guys, just for a moment, okay, and listen to what I have to say with a clear head."

"You are the bad guys!" I cried. "You steal women off the street!"

He shook his head. "Not women. Only you."

I lifted my eyebrows in disbelief. "Only me? Am I supposed to be thankful?"

"No, I just wanted you to know the truth. We're not necessarily the ones you should be afraid of."

"You sure about that? The others shot people. I saw them!"

"They did that for you."

I couldn't stop the laughter bursting from my mouth. "You have got to be kidding me right now."

"Those agents wanted something from you, Darcy."

I locked eyes with him. "You want something from me, too. How does that make you any different?"

He placed a hooked finger against his lips, as though thinking about his answer. "We haven't hurt you, have we?"

"When Alex, Clay, and the others took me, they tied me up. They frightened me."

He rubbed the back of his neck with his whole palm, as though he'd suddenly developed a muscle spasm. "Yes, and I'm sorry for that. But they never did anything more than necessary. And you're right, we do want the same thing, but for a different reason. They would do something bad with it."

I scoffed. "They're the FBI. They're the good guys. They used to work with my dad."

"And yet Michael Sullivan took something from them. They made out like he was the bad guy, too. Had it ever occurred to you that your dad took the memory stick in order to get it out of the wrong hands?"

My teeth dug into my lower lip, biting hard enough to hurt. "I don't know why my dad took it. He was killed before he could tell me anything."

Isaac's head tilted to one side as he regarded me, a wolf assessing whether he should bother slaughtering the lamb. "And the people who killed him also took the flash drive?"

I nodded, but my mind was working fast, trying to piece together exactly what he was telling me. "Yeah, and?"

"The same people who first picked you up, planning to take you down to the headquarters because you let it slip that your dad told you something before he died."

I frowned, confused. "But he didn't. He was barely conscious. That's the saddest part of all this, that he couldn't even tell me he loved me as he died. All he did was repeat a bunch of numbers over and over."

Understanding crashed upon me, and I faltered, blinking hard. The room suddenly felt dizzyingly distant. Blood rushed through my ears, drowning out all other sound, and I took a hitching breath, trying to bring myself back to the moment. The past threatened to open up and swallow me whole.

"You know what those numbers mean, don't you, Isaac?" I managed to say.

He nodded. "Yes. You never mentioned them to anyone before?"

My fingers laced through my hair, tugging hard on the strands. "I didn't think to. It was all a blur, and all I could think about was the blood, and how I was all alone in the world now. Honestly, I didn't give a shit about some flash drive that had been taken or the reasons behind it. I only thought about how I was going to survive. Where I'd live. I can't remember if anyone even asked me if he'd told me anything before he died. Maybe they did, and I told them I didn't remember. I have no idea."

His eyebrows drew together, lines appearing between them in his gravity. "The number your father told you is the code to get access to the information on that drive."

"The code?" Numbers flashed up before me in a firework display of figures.

He nodded. "Yes. Without it, the drive is useless, and the only man who knows how to access it is dead. Almost a week ago, you met with a reporter, and that reporter asked you a very important question. He asked you if your father said anything to you before he died. You told him it had been rubbish, a bunch of numbers that didn't make sense."

"Did someone send the reporter?"

He shook his head. "No, it was pure bad luck. But people have been keeping a close eye on you, Darcy. Always wondering if you knew more than you'd let on. Why did you never tell the FBI that your father had told you a number sequence when he was dying?"

"I didn't know it was a number sequence. Back then, it had just been a blur. I was fourteen. My dad had just died. Why would I have ever thought they were something important? I was just a kid who'd lost her only parent."

His jaw tightened. "We need that code, Darcy."

No, if they wanted something from me, then I wanted information from them, too. "What's on the flash drive?"

"I can't tell you."

"Why not?"

His expression hardened. "I just can't. That knowledge will put you in danger."

I laughed out loud at that. "Don't you think I'm already in enough danger? Your men kidnapped me off the street. People were shot."

"I already told you, you were never in any danger from us. We took you from the men who would have hurt you. But we need that number now, Darcy."

My muscles tightened. "Why?"

"Because we need to access what's on that drive."

"I thought you didn't even have the drive?"

A muscle beside his left eye twitched. "We don't. Not yet. But we will."

"I already told you, my dad just said a jumble of numbers. It was six years ago. How the hell do you expect me to remember?"

"It'll be in your head somewhere. We just need to figure out how to get at them."

I shook my head. "This is crazy."

"No, it isn't. It's necessary. If we don't get those numbers, someone else will find you and take them from you themselves."

I raised my eyebrows in expectation. "And if something happens to me?"

"Then they'll be gone forever, and no one will get access to it."

"My dad took that drive. Maybe he didn't want anyone to have it. Maybe it would be best if something *did* happen to me!"

"No!" His voice hit me like a blast of fire. "Think about it, Darcy. If your dad didn't want anyone to have access to the contents, why would he have told you the numbers? He told you with his dying breath. Does that sound like the actions of a man who didn't want anyone to know what was on it?"

Righteous anger roiled up inside of me, and I straightened my back and lifted my chin. "Yes, he wanted *me* to know what was on it. Not you."

Isaac didn't break his gaze on me, not even for a fraction of a second. "We're the ones who *need* to know."

"It doesn't matter, anyway," I said sullenly. "I already told you, it was a long time ago. I don't even remember them."

He reached out, and I flinched. He paused for a moment, until he knew I was going to hold still, and then leaned in and tapped my temple. "It will be in there somewhere. Something as important as your father's final words won't have left your subconscious so easily, even if you think they have."

I didn't care what he said. I had no intention of ever letting this man have that code. Not that I knew what it was, anyway. What Isaac wasn't considering was that I might not have forgotten the numbers ...

Maybe I had never heard them at all.

"And how do you plan on getting it?" I asked. "It's not like you can open up my head and look inside."

His teeth dug into his lower lip as he regarded me. "No, but there are ways. Your memories aren't stored as we'd imagine, in order, like volumes of encyclopedias on a shelf. They're more like a jigsaw puzzle which is linked together by certain recollections or associations. Sometimes, something as simple as a certain smell can take us back to a childhood memory we were sure we'd forgotten. Only it had never been forgotten, it had simply been stashed away in the long term storage, and then when the scent reminds you, the memory is brought forward into short term, or your working memory. We can try regression, or recall ... hypnosis, even. That memory is in there, Darcy, and I intend to get to it."

I held his gaze, my jaw rigid. "And what if I don't plan on giving it to you?"

"I'm afraid you don't have that option."

"Why? Because you'll kill me?"

"I don't want to threaten you, Darcy."

"Too late. You already have."

He sighed and rubbed a hand over his eyes, as though this whole thing was making him tired. "That isn't my intention. I want you to help us, that's all."

"You want me to help the men who kidnapped me and held me in a cellar for three days?"

"I want you to help the men who took you from people who would have tortured you to get the code out of you. Those were not nice guys, Darcy. Your father knew it, too, that's why he took the flash drive. They were the ones who killed him that night. Not random strangers or criminals, but the same men he worked alongside, day in, day out."

My body trembled. "No, I don't believe you."

He brought his face level with mine. "Why not?"

"Because you have no proof."

He spun around and slammed his hand down on the table. "God-dammit, Darcy. Isn't him taking the flash drive in the first place proof enough? He didn't trust the men he worked with, which is why he took it and protected it with the code. He didn't want them getting access to what's on it."

"What's on it?" I asked again.

"I can't tell you that."

I pressed my lips together, thinking hard. "Okay, then. If getting in-to the flash drive is so important, why didn't you just bring in someone to crack the code? Surely there are people who can hack into just about anything these days?"

Isaac frowned. "It's not that easy. Your father was a smart man and he built a failsafe into the drive where if the number was entered incorrectly, it would wipe everything on the drive."

Wow, my father had some serious faith in my ability to remember, but I guessed that must have been because he knew how my mind worked. "So you need me to remember the numbers exactly right the first time?"

"That's right."

The idea made my head spin. What, even with my ability, I got the numbers wrong? I wasn't sure I could handle that kind of responsibility.

I continued my line of questioning, thirsty for answers. "Who are you guys? Some kind of gang?"

His lips tightened and he glanced away. "You don't need to know what we are."

"Why not? What harm will it do? It's not as though you're going to ever let me tell anyone."

"You don't need to know," he said bluntly, and I scowled at him.

"Then you don't need to know the code."

He huffed out a breath of frustration and stepped away, walking in a small, slow circle in front of me. "I want you to think about this for a while. You're down here, with nowhere to go. No one is going to find you. If you cooperate with us, we'll repay the favor. When we get the drive, and if the code you give us works, you'll be allowed to walk free."

I frowned. "Free? You mean you'll let me live?"

"I keep telling you, we've never meant to hurt you. We just need this, and if we hadn't taken you, those other guys would have."

Was he lying? Was this his way of getting what they wanted, then as soon as they had it, I'd find myself with a bullet in my head?

"Aren't you worried about me going to the cops if you let me go?"

He paused in his movement and lifted his green gaze to mine, solid and confident. "You won't."

"Why not?"

"Because by then you'll have realized that we did the right thing. By then, Darcy, you'll already be on our side."

Chapter Fourteen

I stared at Isaac, at those intense green eyes, and that perfect mouth. Was he serious? Did he really believe I'd ever be on their side? What did he know that I didn't?

Lots. He knew lots. A whole world of knowledge, apparently.

But I was the one who had the most important piece of knowledge stashed somewhere inside my head. And yet he held my freedom, and potentially my life.

So what was more important—that knowledge or my life?

And what if everything he was saying was a lie, and I gave him the number and he killed me anyway? I had to consider that possibility.

"I'll give you some time to think about it," he said, nodding at me as though we'd just conducted a business meeting. Part of me felt as though he was about to try to shake my hand to bring an end to proceedings. "I hope you'll come around to my way of thinking, but as a goodwill gesture, I'll leave you with the light on, and I'll send a couple of the guys down with some food."

"How about as a goodwill gesture, you just let me the hell out of here?"

He gave me a reluctant but-nice-try smile. "You know I can't do that, love. We both know you'd run."

I pressed my lips together, not answering. I didn't need to. He already knew the truth. *Of course I'd run.*

I thought he was going to leave, but instead he moved closer. We were only inches apart now, and the scent of his expensive cologne drifted to my nose.

His tone grew softer and his whole face relaxed. He suddenly looked younger, but only for a moment. "If you escaped, Darcy, where would you go?"

I lifted my head and forced myself to look him directly in the eye. "To the cops. Tell them exactly what you've done."

"And the cops would hand you right over to the FBI."

"So? They might be able to help find all of you."

"Yes, but that wouldn't be what you'd want."

My eyebrows lifted and I tilted my chin. "I promise you it is."

"No, Darcy. They might come to find us, but it wouldn't be for anything to do with punishing us for taking you, not in the way you think. They might try to kill us, but that would be to take us out of the picture. Then they'd do whatever they had to do to get whatever is in your head."

He was talking nonsense, and I huffed in exasperation.

"What I'm saying," he continued, "is that escaping us won't save you. It'll only put you in more danger."

"Right," I said. "Got it. If I escape, I die. If I stay here, but don't give you the code, I'll probably die. So it's all looking good for me, then." I couldn't help the sarcastic bite to my tone.

I didn't miss the twist of amusement at his mouth. "Just think about it, that's all I ask."

He reached out to touch my face, and I slapped his hand away.

"You really are too pretty to die."

Then he turned and left me, closing the door behind him. At least he'd left the light on. I didn't have to stumble around in the dark anymore, and that was something.

With my mind reeling, I sat on the bare mattress of the bed, and put my head in my hands.

There was something Isaac didn't know.

I had a secret. Something only my father had been aware of.

Since as long as I could remember, I was able to see numbers. Not just in my head, but actually visualize numerical sequences in the space around me. I'm a spatial sequence synesthete. It's a form of synesthesia. Where some people's brains processed colors as tastes, or saw days of the week or seasons as certain hues, or musicians may see sounds and music, my brain was able to visualize dates and numbers. I saw the past and future in a timetable of dates. My present was always directly in front of me. My future was to my right, curving around behind me to the point where I could no longer see it. And my past went to my left, again curving behind my head at the point where I could no longer remember.

My dad picked up on my ability when I was only small. How I would always point to my right if I was talking about something in our future or to my left if it was in my past. I'd pretend to pick out numbers from the air, laughing if he'd just walked right through number six or ten. He'd figured it out for me, so, although of course I'd done my own research online, he'd always told me that the way I saw things was different than others. It was almost impossible to explain, and when I was about ten years old, and I'd tried to tell a friend about it, she'd only laughed and gone and told a number of the other girls at school. It had spread quickly, and I'd been taunted for weeks. 'Darcy sees things!' 'Where's today gone, Darcy?' 'Are there numbers dancing around your head!' After that, I'd learned to keep my mouth shut, and I'd learned not to point into the air when I was talking about a date or a number. My memory was good, but it's not photographic as some people would assume when they heard about spatial sequence synesthesia. It was easier to stick to times and dates, and I rarely missed an appointment.

But the point was, my dad knew how numbers worked for me. He knew my affinity for them, and perhaps he thought I'd immediately be able to visualize the code he'd given me and remember. What he hadn't thought about was that I'd been a frightened girl who had her only parent bleeding out into her arms. The last thing I'd been thinking about was visualizing the numbers he'd told me. If I'd known how important they were, perhaps I'd have concentrated a little better.

But I had heard them. They'd gone into my long term memory, whether I liked it or not. But Isaac was wrong about one thing. They wouldn't be in my head. When they came back to me, they'd be right in front of me. So real to me I could reach out my hand and touch them.

I lifted my face from my hands and stared into the air in front of me. Just as I had my whole life, when I thought about certain numbers, they appeared in the bubble of space around me. The number one was closest, and just to the left of my left eye. Eight was behind and slightly above. Three came next, further forward, nearing my nose, and seven was right in the center of my vision. They each had their own particular locations, and if a number was most important to me at that time for some reason, it didn't change position, but instead took on a kind of glow, an illumination that said 'look at me.' I knew this sounded crazy to anyone who hadn't experienced it for themselves, but that was how it had always been to me.

I wondered if my mother had ever experienced synesthesia. From the reading I'd done on the phenomenon, it was often passed down through generations, and I knew it didn't exist on my father's side. But I had no way of knowing. She'd left when I'd been a newborn, vanishing without a trace after telling my dad that she couldn't cope, and being stuck with a baby and a husband wasn't how she'd planned her life to be. He'd tried to stop her, wanting her to get medical help, assuming she was suffering from postpartum depression, but she hadn't wanted it. She hadn't wanted me.

The door opened again, causing me to turn around. Clay walked down the stairs, carrying a tray. Kingsley was not far behind him, though he stood in the doorway, his arms folded across his massive chest, as though daring me to try to get past him.

I offered Clay a conciliatory smile. A part of me still felt if I could get one or more of these guys on my side, they might help me.

"Hey, sugar," he said. "I brought you breakfast."

I got to my feet. Crispy bacon and pancakes, a side of chopped fruit. Coffee and orange juice. It seemed I was living on breakfast right now, but it smelled amazing.

"Thanks, Clay. I'm starving."

"Sorry, no knives and forks. Isaac said you can't be trusted."

I shrugged. "Isaac is probably right."

Clay grinned, revealing a dimple in his cheek. He watched me as I took a seat at the small table and tucked in. I remembered my previous show with the meal he'd given me. I wasn't going to do the same thing again. Not if I wanted to get him on my side. I could feel Kingsley watching me, however, and I wondered if the other man had an idea of what I was thinking. He had a way of doing that, watching, observing, taking in far more than I was willing to give out.

"So," Clay said, leaning casually against the wall beside us. "What do you make of Isaac's proposal?"

I spoke between mouthfuls of salty bacon. "That I give you some mysterious code in return for my freedom?"

"Yeah, that."

I jerked my shoulders. "First of all, I don't even know the code. Isaac thinks there's a way of getting it out of my head, but I'm not sure it's possible."

"It's possible." Kingsley's deep, smooth voice made me look up.

"How would you know?"

"Because I'm a trained therapist in recovering memories."

My eyes widened. "What?"

Clay nodded. "It's true. Kingsley, here, is a shrink."

I hadn't taken these men to be educated to a high level. I'd assumed them to be thugs, criminals. Certainly not a psychologist.

The muscles in my face pulled down in disbelief. "So if Kingsley is a therapist, what do the rest of you do?"

"Alex is a medical doctor."

"Of course, he is." I almost laughed, but held it back. I was stuck in some crazy dream or parallel universe where nothing was what it seemed. "What about you, Clay?"

He held up both hands, and his cheek tweaked. "Nothing so fancy. I'm a mean whizz with an engine, though. There's pretty much nothing I can't make go."

My curiosity built. It didn't sound as though he was lying. Still, it was strange to imagine these guys wandering around, leading regular lives. "And what about Lorcan?"

"He's our weapons guy. Or just fighting in general."

I was almost too scared to ask. "And Isaac?"

"Computers. But he's also the one who makes all the final decisions. We don't always like it, but someone has to, or things wouldn't get done."

"So, you all have regular jobs, and just do a little kidnapping on the side?" My tone was laced with sarcasm and a healthy lashing of bitterness.

Clay exchanged a glance with Kingsley, who gave a shrug.

"Nah, not exactly," said Clay. "We're trained in those things, but we don't work regular jobs. I mean, Kingsley doesn't have his own practice or anything, and neither does Alex, but they were both put through training."

I picked up on something he'd said. "They were put through training? By who?"

That same glance exchanged again, a silent communication about what could and couldn't be said.

Clay rubbed his fingers across his lips, as though he'd suddenly found something on them. "Sorry. Can't tell you that."

I didn't think he was lying. Who the hell were these people? I was starting to see them all with new eyes. Psychologist, mechanic, weapons, doctor, technology. This wasn't a group of uneducated criminals. Okay, they were still criminals—kidnapping me had proven that—but they weren't stupid.

And they wanted to get inside my head.

What could be on that drive? What were they after? The reports after my father died simply said he'd taken classified information. I was never told what that information was, and of course he didn't talk about what he was working on with his fourteen-year-old daughter.

Remembering my half-eaten breakfast, I picked up a pancake and chomped down. The pancake was light and fluffy, and sweet, and reminded me of Saturday mornings with my dad when I'd been younger. The ultimate comfort food. Considering I didn't know when I'd be getting my next meal—hell, this could even be my last meal—I didn't plan on letting anything go to waste.

I swallowed my mouthful then circled my finger in the air to indicate all of them. "So, who is the cook?"

Clay held up his hand as though volunteering for something in class. "That'd be me as well."

I hadn't expected it to be him, for some reason, though I always did like the idea of a guy who could cook. I burned toast and boiled eggs dry. I guessed I couldn't take anything for granted. There was Kingsley, looking like he could crack your neck with a single finger, but actually more interested in the mind than being physical. I remembered the massage and shivered, and not in a bad way. Okay, maybe he did like to get hands on as well, only not in the violent way I'd assumed. Alex had patched up my wounds, because that was what he was trained to do, but I still got the feeling he didn't like to see me hurt. Lorcan, I hadn't figured out at all yet, and I didn't even know where to start with Isaac.

But if I agreed to what they wanted, maybe I would get some answers.

Chapter Fifteen

I finished eating and gave a contented sigh.

I suddenly realized something. At some point, though I couldn't put my finger on the exact moment, I'd stopped being afraid of these guys. Isaac, yeah, perhaps. And I hadn't warmed to Lorcan. But I didn't hate Clay, Kingsley, and Alex in the way I had when I'd first been brought here. Was Stockholm syndrome coming into play, and I was forming a bond with my captors, or was I actually starting to believe some of what they were telling me? Maybe those FBI agents who had come to pick me up had been bad news, though I'd known one of them, Agent Hollan, for years. I remembered how brusque he'd been with me, how I hadn't been able to grab my purse, and I'd barely had time to put my shoes on. I hadn't felt comfortable with them either, but then I hadn't expected to. I'd been feeling horrible about the interview, part of me wishing I could give the money back and forget I'd ever opened my mouth. I certainly wished I'd gone down that route now. Look at the amount of shit my big mouth and greed had gotten me into.

It was all about those numbers my dad had told me as he'd died. If he hadn't wanted me to access the files on that drive, why would he have told me the number? If he'd wanted whatever was on it to die with him, he could have kept his mouth shut, or told me he loved me, like any normal father would have done.

My curiosity had gotten the better of me. Even if I was able to walk away from this right now, I'd still want to know. Perhaps the men would never tell me what was on the drive, but unless we figured out the code, and they did the job of getting their hands on it, I would never find out.

"Okay," I said eventually.

Clay looked at me quizzically, one eyebrow cocked. "Okay?"

"Tell Isaac I'll do it."

A grin spread across Clay's face and he looked up to Kingsley, who gave a slow nod. The man wasn't demonstrative in emotion, but I could tell he was pleased. That I'd done something to make them happy caused a warm glow of approval to spread through me. I tried to shake the feeling off. I knew that was a dangerous road to go down. They were the enemies.

Weren't they?

Clay reached across me and picked up my empty tray. I started to get to my feet, too, but he frowned at me. "What are you doing?"

"Coming with you. I'm helping you now. I'm on your side. Surely that means I don't have to be locked down here anymore."

Clay's mouth twisted and he shook his head. "Sorry, sweetheart. No can do. Maybe if you hadn't run yesterday, and cut up Isaac, I could have convinced him, but right now he still thinks you're going to run at the first opportunity."

"And he's probably right," Kingsley called down from the top of the stairs.

I lifted both hands in exasperation. "Aww, come on!"

"Sorry, sugar," said Clay. "But play your cards right, and who knows what will happen." He held my gaze, teasing laughter dancing behind his eyes. Was he flirting with me? How could he be flirting when I was essentially their prisoner? I forced myself to hold his gaze, trying to be challenging rather than flirty, though I felt my cheeks heat. In the end, Clay gave me a wink then turned away, still holding the tray, to join Kingsley at the top of the stairs.

"I'll tell Isaac," Kingsley called back down to me. "I doubt he'll want to wait long to get started. Prepare yourself."

I opened my mouth to ask him what I was supposed to do to prepare myself, but the door shut and the lock clicked back into place before I got the chance. I felt better, physically, since getting something to eat and drink. I felt stronger mentally, too. Even though I'd been effectively blackmailed into cooperating, I was doing something to take control of my situation. I was a part of this now—though I still wasn't completely sure of what was going on.

I went to the bathroom to brush my teeth and splash a little water on my face. In front of the mirror, I raked my hands through my hair, still knotted from where it had dried without me combing it the previous day. There were tiny nicks on my forehead where splinters of glass must have caught my face when I'd charged through the broken window. I pressed my lips together to hold back a manic laugh. No wonder the men didn't trust what I was going to do. I looked like a crazy woman.

The thought of delving into the day of my father's death caused nerves to tumble around my guts like laundry inside a dryer. I knew I'd blocked a lot of it out. Maybe it had been from shock, or simply because it had happened years ago, my memories of that day were blurred. Only when I dreamed about them did they become clear, but they faded again as soon as I woke. The idea of facing it all head on, of experiencing it all over again, made me feel sick. But I wasn't a coward, and I truly believed my father would have wanted me to remember. He had told me for a reason. He'd told me because he'd thought that with my number synesthesia I would remember what he'd said. Perhaps he'd even thought I would have been able to visualize it. I'd already let him down by forgetting.

I wished Isaac would tell me exactly what was on the flash drive, though. I debated holding back until he told me, but he already had my freedom and my life hanging over me. If I told him I wouldn't do it until he gave me that information, we'd be at a stalemate, and I'd be left down here to rot. No, I had to cooperate. Perhaps if the men all thought I was on their side they'd trust in me more. They might let me out of the cellar, and, in time, might even tell me what was so important about that drive. I just hoped giving them the information wasn't me signing someone else's death warrant.

Chapter Sixteen

I'd barely had time to get myself together when the door opened again. I hadn't been expecting all of the men to come down, but it appeared that was what was happening. Isaac led the way, with Kingsley close behind. Next was Alex, and then Clay. Lorcan came last, and he locked the door, as though I stood any chance of getting past all five of them. Locking the door again showed me that they didn't quite trust me yet. They weren't stupid, and they knew I could have said I'd help simply to get them on my side.

Isaac spoke first. "Kingsley told me the good news. I'm pleased to hear you're willing to cooperate."

"I don't think you've given me much choice," I replied.

He ducked his head slightly in a nod of acknowledgment. "Maybe not, but I hope you'll come to see it's the right thing to do."

"So do I."

I looked around at the others. Lorcan stared at me, his dark eyes slightly narrowed, as though he didn't trust me. Alex was watching me, too, and I gave him a small smile, hoping he was on my side.

"How are the cuts?" he asked.

I looked down at my arms and thumbed one of the Band-Aids. They didn't hurt too much at all now. "Better, thanks."

Clay took a seat on the stairs, his arms slung casually around his knees, as though he was only here for the entertainment.

Something occurred to me, and I cast my gaze down to the men's pockets. Did one of them have a cell phone? There was a good chance. If I could get close enough to steal a phone, I could call for help when they'd all gone back upstairs. I wished I knew how to pickpocket. I imagined I'd have to get one of them close then distract them somehow, while slipping my hand inside their pocket and hoping they didn't notice me taking the phone. I had an idea of what I might need to do to distract them, and how close that would mean I'd have to get to one of them. The thought made me shiver. I didn't want to do that, but I would, if that was what it took to save my life. Of course, I didn't have an address or anything I could tell the cops, even if I was able to make a call, but I was sure they were able to track cell phones these days.

"Right," said Isaac, distracting me from my plotting. "Shall we get started?"

Kingsley moved forward. "Where do you feel the most comfortable to sit?" he asked me.

I glanced at the others. "Are we going to do this with everyone watching?"

"We need to be here," said Alex. "We need to hear what you have to say. One of us might miss something important."

"But does it need all five of you?"

"We work as a team," said Isaac. "Each one of us is as important as the other. I won't exclude them from this."

"I ... just ..."

His eyebrows lifted expectantly. "We could film it instead, to watch later, if that would make you more comfortable."

"No, it wouldn't!" I didn't want to be filmed. What if I did or said something embarrassing, only for it to be immortalized on film? They'd be able to do anything with it. Post it on social media for it to go viral. I could end up as a YouTube star or something equally as hideous.

I sighed, giving in, then gestured to my little cubby under the stairs. "I guess this is where I feel most comfortable."

Kingsley nodded, but fine lines appeared between his brows as he frowned. "It'll be a squash, but I guess we can work with that."

Oh, damn. It hadn't occurred to me that Kingsley would be coming into the cubby with me. With his massive frame, we'd certainly be getting cozy. Not that I minded being too close to Kingsley. I still remembered the feel of his strong fingers massaging cream into my back. Now there might be a chance he was actually one of the good guys, I couldn't stop my mind from straying, wondering if there might be any chance of a repeat performance.

Feeling self-conscious, I ducked down and crawled into my cubby, wedging myself in the corner closest to the stairs, so I could give Kingsley the side with the most space. He climbed in after me and sat down, twisting to face me. His pants legs stretched across his massive thighs, and I did my best not to check out the lines of muscles beneath, or anything else the material might be stretched across in that particular area.

I heard a scrape and glanced over to see Isaac dragging the chair so he could take a seat in front of us. He twisted the chair around so the back faced the stairs then swung his leg over to sit on it back to front. I also didn't miss how this position stretch the material of the expensive suit pants he wore. Dammit. What was wrong with my mind today? Was I trying to distract myself from the inevitable, or was the possibility that these guys weren't all bad making me see them in a different light?

Having Isaac sitting there was intimidating, though.

"Do you have to do that?" I asked, my eyebrows raised.

His lips pursed slightly, his eyes narrowing. "Do what?"

"Sit like you're about to bring out the popcorn."

"Sorry, love." He didn't sound in the slightest bit sorry, and I didn't miss the smirk pulling at the corners of his mouth. He lifted the chair and dragged it back a couple of feet. "This any better?"

"S'pose," I grumbled.

Kingsley reached out and touched my leg, making me jump. "Focus on me," he said. "Ignore the others in the room. Within a few minutes, you'll have forgotten they're even here."

Somehow, I highly doubted that.

Even so, I turned to Kingsley so we both sat cross-legged, facing each other. He was surprisingly supple for such a big man. He looked into my face, focusing all his attention on me. He had the aura of being someone you could trust, and together with that deep, melodic voice, I could see why he chose the career route he did.

Nerves jangled inside me like a cymbal crashing. There was so much about this situation I felt uncomfortable with, I barely knew how to process it.

Was I really about to allow Kingsley into my head? What if he used the hypnosis to make me do things I wouldn't normally do? What if he put the thought into my head that I didn't want to leave this place? He could make me compliant just by suggesting it.

I put out my hand to stop him. "Hang on a minute."

He mirrored my movement, so our fingers were almost touching. "I'm not going to make you walk around quacking like a duck, if that's what you're worried about."

I hated that he could read me so well. I guessed it came with the job.

My mind spun, trying to think of all the things that made me so paranoid about doing this. "What about false memory? What if you plant something in there that isn't real and it changes my whole perception on life?"

My tone had been growing higher as my outburst mounted, and Kingsley frowned at me with a quizzical look that contained humor. "You've either been watching too many television shows, or else reading the wrong books."

"Okay, then," I tried again. "What if you make me remember, and I tell you the code, and then you make me completely forget it again? So you'll know it, and I won't."

"Again, fiction. You remembering will take time. It won't be done in one session. I need to take you back to that night, and it's going to be done through several different ways. We'll walk through the events, step by step. We'll use sound and smells to try to form a link between your long term and short term memory. It's not like I'm going to put you under and '*bam*' there is the code. Plus, you'll remember everything we say and do. You won't be unconscious, but more in a dream-like state, or super relaxed."

"Like I just smoked a joint?" I suggested, doubtfully, trying to figure out what it would feel like.

He laughed. "Kinda."

"Okay."

"First of all," he said, "I want you to regulate your breathing. Breathe slowly in through your nose and out through your mouth. Think about how your lungs expand as you take that breath, and how you relax again as you breathe it out."

I did as he'd asked, inhaling slowly and back out again. I kept my eyes locked on his, trying to forget the four other men in the room.

"Good," he said. "Now close your eyes."

I allowed my eyelids to slip shut, plunging me into darkness, but Kingsley's voice kept me present, giving me something to concentrate on.

"Continue to breathe. With each exhalation your body will find a deeper relaxation all of its own."

He was right. I was relaxed, more than I had since being taken, perhaps even long before then. My shoulders had been hunched up to my ears, but as I continued to breathe, they eased down.

"Imagine you can see a screen on the backs of your eyelids," Kingsley said, "like a big movie screen that's taking up the whole of your vision."

To my surprise, that was exactly what I could see. A big cinema screen right in front of me.

"What can you see on the screen?" he asked.

"Nothing." I spoke, but my voice sounded distant. "It's white with static."

"Okay. Good. Now, I want you to think about the day your father died. Can you do that?"

I nodded.

"Imagine you're watching the events happening on the screen in front of you. What's the first thing you remember about that night?"

"My dad and I were fighting. I wanted to go to a party, and he wouldn't let me go because I'd stayed out past my curfew a few nights earlier."

"Good. Can you see that on the screen?"

The screen flickered, and, as though I was watching a television show of my own life, I saw myself appear. I was facing away, so I could only see my back, but I was able to see my father. My heart lurched with a combination of love, pain, regret, and grief, strong enough to snatch my breath.

In the outside world, Kingsley must have noticed. "Keep breathing, Darcy. Nice and slowly. In through your nose, out through your mouth."

I tried to remember to breathe, while keeping my eyes glued on my father on the screen.

I didn't keep photos of him around the house for this exact reason. It hurt me to think of him, and I preferred to tough things out rather than be caught out at unsuspecting moments by walking past a framed photograph of him I'd forgotten about. On the movie screen, his face was contorted with anger and he was pointing a finger in my direction. He still wore his work suit, and the glass patio doors were directly behind him, darkness lying beyond.

I desperately wanted to interact, to stand up and shout at my dad to be careful, and get away from the doors. But I was quite literally an observer in all of this, and there was nothing more I could do but watch events unfold.

"Tell me what's happening," Kingsley said, his voice only just coming through to me. I opened my mouth to speak, feeling as though I was drunk and not completely in control of my body.

"We're fighting," I said. "I'm shouting at him, telling him I hate him and that he's ruining my life because he won't let me go out."

"Good. Keep watching."

My voice came out as a whisper. "I don't want to."

"You have to, Darcy. We need to know."

A flash of movement came from behind my father, a glimpse through the glass frames of the door. I hadn't noticed it on the night he'd died, or at least I thought I hadn't, but if I was able to see it now, I must have spotted the movement on a subconscious level. I'd just been too caught up in my own selfish problems that I hadn't registered it properly and been able to warn him.

I wanted to tell my father to run. I wanted to reach out and grab him, pull him out of harm's way, but I wasn't there.

The floor beneath my feet started to move, slipping beneath me so the distance between myself and the screen decreased. No, that was wrong. The ground wasn't moving, it was me who was moving. Some unseen force dragged me toward the screen.

I hadn't realized before that I'd been seated. As though I was sitting in my own personal movie theatre. My hands gripped the armrests of the chair, my knuckles white. I didn't know what I was supposed to do.

"No!" I cried. "Help!"

Kingsley's voice, so distant I could barely hear him. "Darcy, what's wrong?"

I was dragged closer and closer, and nothing I did could change anything. The screen was sucking me in. And I could hear Kingsley's voice, concerned now, but I couldn't connect to it.

An audible *pop* sounded in my ears, and I found myself no longer watching the memory from a distance. I was in it. I was the Darcy I'd been watching on screen, and my father was standing in front of me.

I opened my mouth to scream at him to watch out, but the *thwack thwack* of two silenced gunshots made me jerk back. My dad staggered forward, and automatically, I held out my arms for him to fall into.

"Nooooo!"

A scream of anguish pealed from my throat. The cry was for two reasons—that my father had been shot, and that I'd known it was going to happen and had been powerless to stop it.

Chapter Seventeen

I staggered to the floor with my father's weight, so he lay, bleeding out in my lap, looking up at me with wide, frightened eyes. It was happening again. My dad was dying, and there was nothing I could do about it.

Panic squeezed my chest, causing my lungs to constrict, my heart beating so fast and hard, I was sure it would explode. Blood. Blood everywhere. All over my hands, under my nails. Seeping into my clothes. How was it possible for one person to contain so much blood? I felt like I was drowning in it and I would never escape.

In the back of my mind, I knew none of this was real, yet it felt real in that moment. I was aware of Kingsley calling my name, but he sounded miles away. I couldn't break out of the events of my past. I knew I was supposed to be listening to what my father was saying to me, but red painted my vision. *Dying, dying, dying, dying...*

My thoughts jumbled, trying to piece together my experiences.

It is his blood, isn't it? Not mine? Or is it mine? Has something happened to me, too? My mind blurred, trying to distinguish what was real and what was part of my vision. *I'm in trouble. Men have taken me, I'm sure of it. There has been shooting. Had I been shot as well?* My mind turned over fragments of thought, but I was caught in a blind rush of panic and terror, not wanting to believe what was happening, while unable to deny it.

In the real world, Kingsley continued trying to bring me back, but I'd plunged too far down the rabbit hole. I fought him, thrashing against hands meant to calm me, my body reacting independently of my mind. I only wanted to get away. I had forgotten I was locked down in a cellar and I had nowhere else to go.

Back in the cellar, I scrambled to my feet.

In my head, I remained in the living room of my house, my father dying on the floor. I knew this wasn't what had happened in real life, but perhaps that was why I felt the need to run so badly. I couldn't cling to the hope that he would be all right, because I knew that he hadn't been. He had died, and he was dying now. Was it my fault? Could I have done more? And yet here, I was running away. There was something else I was supposed to be doing, but the blood was everywhere, and I couldn't breathe. I only wanted to get away and escape.

I was vaguely aware of chaos in the cellar, of me fighting the men, of not listening to anything anyone was saying. How could Kingsley bring me back when I couldn't hear him over the blood rushing through my ears and the galloping hooves of my heartbeat?

Then a body pushed me backward, up against the wall behind me, pinning me against it. Strong and determined. I was still lost in my personal hell, but the pressure of the body seemed to calm me, like a weighted blanket. In my head, I began to calm, the blood still terrifying me, but my determination to run seeping from my body.

"Darcy, come back to me now."

Kingsley's voice, closer now.

Was that who was pressed up against me?

The scent of leather replaced the iron tang of blood. A strong, hard body took over the limp bleeding one in my arms.

"It's all right, princess," a voice growled. "You're all right. You're safe."

I blinked my eyes, and my bloodied living room vanished. I found myself staring into a set of intense dark eyes. Dark brows and a dimple in his chin. Lorcan. His body pressed firm against mine. The scent of him—leather and something musky—washed over me. He was several inches taller than I was, and I felt his chest heave as I caught my breath.

He stared down into my eyes, holding me in his gaze. The memories of the blood and trauma fled, and all I could think about was this man's body, how his chest moved in time with mine, my breasts pushed up against him. Of all the guys I'd have expected to help me, he would have been the last one I'd put my money on, and yet here he was.

Perhaps I was just trying to erase the thought of blood from my mind, but I stood on tiptoes and my arms found their way around his neck. Lorcan seemed as caught in the moment as I was. Not needing any further encouragement, he ducked down and crushed his mouth to mine, his body slamming against me. His tongue slipped into my mouth, and we were kissing and kissing, and I could feel his desire for me wedged hard against my hip.

I knew the others were there, watching, and yet it didn't embarrass me. If anything, it only made me hotter, the thought of the four guys watching as Lorcan and I made out against the wall.

What the hell was wrong with me?

"Lorcan," came Isaac's voice. "That's enough."

Was Isaac pissed? Had he wanted to be the first? The thought surprised me. Had I really thought like that? Did each of the men have a claim on me? I was their captive, after all, but though the thought should have filled me with revulsion, I felt a flutter of excitement stir inside me. Would they pass me around, one by one, or would they take me all at once?

"I think we may be losing focus here," said Kingsley, from just behind Isaac.

Lorcan and I parted, and a hot blush crawled up my throat. I didn't know what had come over me, and I worried the men could read my thoughts on my face. Kingsley had always been particularly good at that.

Isaac stepped forward. "What did you see? Did you remember the number?"

I felt like I'd let them all down. Like I'd failed.

"It was the same as I remembered. My dad being shot then all the blood, and I'd panicked." I paused and shook my head briefly. "No, it had been worse in the memory. I didn't even hear him say the numbers."

"Dammit." Isaac turned to Kingsley. "Do it again."

My stomach dropped at the thought of having to experience my father's death all over again.

But Kingsley shook his head. "No, she's done enough. She needs a break."

I offered Kingsley a grateful smile, thankful I had someone on my side.

Alex stepped forward. "We can't do that again. Look at the state of her." He was always the one most protective of me. Was that because he was a medical doctor, and so it was in his profession to be caring, or was it something more? I didn't miss the irony that he was the one who'd first grabbed me, and it was his nose I'd kicked.

"Yes, we can," said Isaac. "We were almost there."

"She's too suggestible," said Kingsley. For some reason, I couldn't help feeling embarrassed at being suggestible, as though it showed a weakness in my character that I had no control over. "When I took her under, she went too deep, and I couldn't get her out again."

Isaac's eyes narrowed. "Isn't there something we can do to stop her going so far under?"

"If we want her to remember, she needs to be under," said Kingsley. "What we need to work on is her recall, bringing her back out again."

"Lorcan kissing her seemed to work," Clay called out.

My face flamed with heat, but it hadn't been the kissing, not really, though it had helped. "It was the physical contact," I said. "Him pressing up against me. It calmed me enough to hear Kingsley's voice again and reconnect with the real world."

Kingsley looked to the others and then nodded. "Physical contact. That can work."

"Do we get to volunteer for who goes first?" Clay called, teasing in his tone

I flipped him the bird and tried to hold back the tugging of a smile at the corners of my mouth. Having Clay pressed up against me didn't seem like such a bad thing either.

These are the bad guys, remember, Darcy?

Nothing they were doing was for me. The only reason they'd stepped in with the Feds was because they wanted the same thing from me as the agents. If they hadn't, they'd have left me to my fate. These men didn't give a shit about me. They were only interested in what was in my head.

"I don't care what we have to do," said Isaac with a frown. "We need that code. Time's running out."

Kingsley nodded. "And we'll get it, but if we traumatize her, we risk her pushing the memory further back in her mind, and it'll be even harder for her to pull it into her conscious mind."

Isaac glanced over at me, still standing up against the wall. I felt like I should say something and plead my case, but it didn't matter what I said. These men were deciding everything.

"Okay, fine." He turned to me. "Get some rest. We'll try again after you've had a break. This isn't something we can just let go."

I nodded. "Yeah, I figured as much."

Clay pushed himself up from where he'd been sitting on the stairs, and turned to trot back up. Alex followed, and then the others.

One person lurked behind.

Lorcan stopped in front of me, a troubled expression on his face. Almost in an unconscious gesture, he reached out and brushed his fingers against mine. I tried not to be distracted by the tattoos running up the side of his neck.

"Hey, I'm sorry about what happened back there."

I feigned innocence. "You mean pulling me out of the hypnosis?"

"I mean kissing you."

The way he was looking at me was too intense, and I closed my eyes briefly to break the moment and look away. The way I remembered it, I was the one who'd instigated the kiss, but perhaps I was wrong. "I think considering you guys are my kidnappers, one of you kissing me isn't the biggest wrong you've done me."

He frowned and nodded, his lips pressed together. "Yeah, but kidnapping you needed to be done for your own safety. What I did was just a reaction."

I looked up at him. I don't know why I wanted to make him feel better, but I did. "It's fine, Lorcan. You helped. I was stuck in a nightmare, and you knew what to do to bring me out of it."

The frown hadn't quite left his face. "We're okay, then?"

"As much as a captive can be with one of her captors."

His teeth nipped his lower lip and he glanced away. "I wish you didn't think of us that way."

"How else am I supposed to think of you? I'm a prisoner here. You won't let me leave."

He brought his hazel eyes back to mine. "We want you to work with us."

"I am," I argued, "and you still won't let me out of this damned cellar."

"Isaac will come around. Just cooperate, and things will get better."

I cocked my eyebrows. "Sounds an awful lot like kidnapped talk to me."

He rubbed his hand over his mouth. "Shit, yeah. It does, doesn't it?"

"Were you guys sent on some kind of course before taking me?"

I surprised a laugh out of him. It was the first time I'd seen Lorcan crack so much as a smile, and I found myself staring at his mouth, remembering what his lips had felt like pressed against mine, his tongue pushing into my mouth, hot and heavy. And even as Lorcan had been kissing me, a part of me had been aware of the others, too, standing, watching.

Shit, I was bonding with them. Well, not Isaac, but maybe the others. Connecting with them like in the syndrome. I knew it was wrong, but I couldn't help it. In this world of darkness, they were giving me something to hold onto. They made me feel excited about something again, where I'd lived my life plodding mundanely through each day since my father had been killed. Now I had a purpose, though it may only last until I remembered the code. Then they'd have no use for me.

Shit, why hadn't I thought of that before? If I gave them the code, what would stop them from killing me?

"What's wrong?" Lorcan asked, his dark eyebrows converging.

"Nothing. I'm just tired. I need to sleep." A yawn, conjured by my mention of sleep, tugged at my jaw, but I swallowed it down.

His chin tilted to one side. "But we're okay?"

"Sure."

It was all I could think of to say. He was kind of sweet, in a moody, tattooed, kidnapper way.

But whatever happened, when I remembered that code, I couldn't just give it to them. I didn't know what was on that memory stick, but I planned on being around long enough to find out.

Chapter Eighteen

The men left me alone for a few hours.

I didn't like being trapped with only my thoughts. At least the guys were a distraction—some of them not such a great distraction, though I was starting to warm to the others, despite my internal advice to myself to stay well clear.

Memories of the day my dad died went around my head. Did I think I could have saved him? I'd only been fourteen, and unarmed against men who'd clearly come to our home with murder on their minds. And yet I wondered if there had been more I could have done. If I'd pressed my hand to the bullet wounds, would he have lost less blood and survived? If I'd not been arguing with him about not being allowed out that night, would he have been in a different room, his back not exposed to the gunman? There were so many 'what ifs,' and I knew there was nothing I could do about it now, but that didn't stop my mind from turning them over and over.

The thought of having to go back into those memories made my stomach churn with nerves. What if I remembered the numbers he'd told me, and, while I was under, I spoke them out loud? Would the guys kill me? I wouldn't put it past Isaac, but the others? Would they do something to stop him, or was I completely misreading the situation? One minute, they showed me a hint of softness peeping through those rock hard exteriors, and the next second they shut down on me.

Were the others as cold-hearted as Isaac, and I was simply projecting a gentleness onto them to try to convince myself I'd survive all of this?

Going through the hypnosis had sapped me of energy, so I took up my spot under the stairs and quickly fell asleep.

I WOKE TO THE DOOR opening again. Blinking open sleep-sticky eyes, I saw all of the guys had returned.

Isaac stood over me, his arms folded. The sleeves of his white shirt were rolled up, exposing the gauze and tape covering the spot where I'd slashed him with the razor. "Ready to try this again?"

"Can I wake up properly first?"

Clay's head appeared behind Isaac's shoulder. "Hey, sugar. I made you a sandwich. Coffee, too."

I climbed out, ignoring Isaac. "Thanks."

"How are you feeling?" Alex stood with his hands shoved into the pockets of his pants, his expression serious.

"A bit shaken up from having to re-live everything, but otherwise okay."

"Your mental health is as important to look after as your physical one." Kingsley said from where he was lurking near the bed.

I opened my mouth to comment on how being kidnapped and held in a cellar for three days wasn't much good for either my mental or physical health, but I managed to trap the words on my tongue. I was playing the good girl now, being cooperative. As far as I could tell, it was my only chance at getting out of here in one piece.

Instead I just shrugged and looked back to Alex. "Sure."

Alex's lips tightened, a muscle in his temple twitching. He must have picked up on my reluctance. "You feel ready to try again, or not?"

I took a deep breath, filling my lungs. "I can do it."

I wasn't going to plunge into my past just yet, though. First, I was going to eat my damned sandwich. For all I knew, it might be the last thing I ever ate.

The men's eyes followed me as I moved to the table and picked the sandwich off the plate. I didn't want to let them intimidate me, but it was hard not to feel self-conscious when under such scrutiny. I took a bite, chewing methodically, trying to prove to both myself and the men that I wouldn't be rushed. The chair was beside me, and I debated whether or not to sit down. Sitting made me feel more vulnerable, while standing made me look awkward. In the end, I sank into the seat, finishing up the food and downing the coffee.

Isaac turned to the others. "Okay, while Darcy is eating, we need to come up with a plan for if she goes too far under again. Who's going to bring her out of it, if Kingsley can't?"

I glanced to Lorcan. Was he going to volunteer again? He remained quiet, and I couldn't help but feel rejected. Did he still regret the kiss, or feel bad about it? I found it strange how someone who'd helped kidnap me could feel badly about kissing me.

"Hey, I'll be happy to help," volunteered Clay. I couldn't stop myself smiling at him, but Isaac raised a hand.

"No, Alex, you do it."

"No fair," protested Clay.

"Alex is more likely to control himself," Isaac said.

I lifted my eyebrows. Was Isaac worried Clay would push himself up against me and not be able to stop? I'd thought Lorcan kissing me hadn't bothered him, but now I wondered.

"That's fine," said Alex, as though he'd just been asked to run to the grocery store rather than get up close and personal with me. "I can do it."

Kingsley turned to me. "Let's get started, then."

"You want me to go back in the cubby?"

"No, you're suggestible. I think you'll go under easily wherever you are."

Great.

I twisted in my chair to face him. The others stood around, Alex the closest, Isaac not far behind, Clay already sitting on the bed. Lorcan had put the most distance between us, remaining near the stairs. The food I'd just eaten swirled uncomfortably around in my stomach, churning with nerves, and I clenched my fists, trying to control my feelings. I didn't want to have to go through it all again, but what choice did I have?

Kingsley crouched in front of me. "Remember how I told you to regulate your breathing?" I nodded. "Good. Let's do that again."

I complied, breathing long and slow in through my nose and out through my mouth, feeling my chest expand and my shoulders start to drop. Automatically, my eyes slipped shut, and I focused in on Kingsley's voice.

"I want you to go back to that day again, Darcy. The day your father died. I want you to remember that you're only an observer in this situation. You are watching and listening and learning. You are not involved, do you understand? You can't affect what is happening, and you're not really there. Okay?"

I nodded.

"Can you see the screen in front of you again?"

It appeared on the backs of my eyelids as soon as he said the words, and I dipped my chin again to tell him I could.

The chair was more solid beneath me this time, the velvet fabric beneath my fingertips as I clutched the arms, trying to root myself on this side of the screen.

Kingsley's deep voice filtered through to me. "On screen, you're watching the night your father died. You're just an observer. You cannot interact in any way. Do you understand?"

My heart beat grew faster, and I could feel my breathing speed up as well.

"Stay calm, Darcy. Control your breathing. In through your nose, out through your mouth."

On screen, my past self was fighting with my dead father. My eyes went to the dark glass doors beyond him. I fought my desperation to do something to help, and even though my eyes were shut in the real world, they welled with tears, trembling beneath my eyelashes and spilling down my cheeks.

An observer. I'm an observer.

I wanted to be there, to help, to *do* something! But all I could do was watch, and yet I didn't want to. I didn't want to watch my father die again. I didn't even want to see the anger on his face as he argued with my teenage self. My gaze drifted away, drawn toward the darkened panes of the door once more.

That flash of movement came again.

My heart lurched.

What did I just see? Someone there? Did I see my father's killer?

My focus was suddenly renewed. It had almost been nothing—a flash of light. And then my father staggered forward as the bullets punched through his back, with enough force to penetrate right through his torso, and the Darcy on screen stepped forward to catch him as he fell.

I knew the men who'd taken me wanted me to listen to the words my father was muttering as he lay dying in my arms, but my mind was on something else. I'd seen who'd killed him. What else had my subconscious picked up on?

My gaze darted around, frantic, terrified I'd miss something.

There! A reflection in the glass. Someone standing just out of view, but reflected in the glass.

My heart stopped, and I burst out of my hypnosis, gasping and clutching at anything real. Alex was there, pulling me into his arms, giving me something solid to hang onto.

"What is it, Darcy?" came Isaac's clipped English accent. "Did you get the code?"

I shook my head. "No." The man's face stayed fresh in my mind. "I saw the man who killed my father."

Kingsley frowned. "Who?"

"Agent Hollan. The same man who took me from the house the morning you kidnapped me."

Chapter Nineteen

That Agent Hollan was my father's killer left me reeling.

Lyle Hollan had been the closest thing to Michael Sullivan's partner as you could get in the FBI. He'd been by my father's side every step of the way, had come to our place for cook-outs and watched football games with us. He'd argued my father's case as best he could after all the accusations about my father taking sensitive material, and had stood at Aunt Sarah's side during his funeral. That he was the same man who'd shot those bullets through the glass filled me with fury. After my father, Michael's, death, Hollan had distanced himself from our family. I hadn't given it much thought. I figured he had his own life to get on with, and why would he want to be saddled with Aunt Sarah and me? I wasn't exactly an easy teenager.

But I had trusted him, and, more importantly, my *father* had trusted him. Or had he? Had he known at that point that Hollan wasn't all he seemed? If so, why hadn't he warned me?

With the knowledge of who had killed my father came something else. Hollan must have also been the one to take the memory stick my father had encrypted with the code, and if these guys didn't have the stick, but they wanted the code, they must know a way of getting it.

"So you believe us now?" said Isaac, though he didn't have any satisfaction in his tone. He straightened his shirt sleeves. "You see we're not the bad guys."

I still didn't know about that. Maybe not the others, but Isaac wasn't someone I trusted. "You could have just told me all of this. Come to my house and explained."

"I already told you, there wasn't time. We didn't know you'd be in any danger until that interview was published and you talked about the numbers, and then it was a race to who got to you first. Hollan did, and we had to take the appropriate action."

"Killing them, and kidnapping me."

At least I could take some pleasure in the knowledge my father's murderer was dead, even if he hadn't been brought to justice, his name smeared in the dirt, as my father's had been.

"We didn't kill all of them."

"What?"

Deep down, I already knew what he was going to say.

"Hollan got away. Our priority was with you, and he made a run for it."

"So he's still out there?"

I remembered how it had felt when I'd seen Hollan at the front door that morning, how the shame at selling my father's story had filled me, how his ex-best friend was now about to tell me what a terrible person I was. I'd hated myself in that moment, when my emotions had been directed in completely the wrong direction. My body tensed as I relived that fateful morning, and what I would have done if I'd known the truth back then. My rage made me wish I'd picked up the kitchen knife and met Hollan with it at the front door. I imagined plunging the blade into his gut, the surprise on his face, and the pleasure I would have felt at telling him that I knew exactly what he'd done. I had it in me to kill him. I knew I did.

"Darcy?" Alex reached out to touch the back of my hand. "Are you all right? You're shaking."

I glanced down at where our hands made contact. He was right, I was trembling all over, but it wasn't with fear, it was with anger.

"You don't need to keep me locked up down here," I said. "I'm with you on whatever you guys want to do. I want to find the son of a bitch and kill him, and if giving you the code pisses Hollan off and goes against whatever the hell he's planning, then I'm all for it."

Alex twisted his head and looked toward Isaac. I noticed the others exchanging glances, too. I guessed this wasn't a decision they were able to make right away.

"I'm not going to fight you," I tried again. "I'm on your side. Do whatever you want with me afterward. I don't care. The only thing I care about is Hollan getting what's coming to him."

Kingsley looked to Isaac. "I believe her."

"I do, too." Lorcan had remained his usual quiet self by the stairs, but took the moment to speak.

Clay threw me a wink. "My vote goes with baby-doll."

I scowled at him for the name, especially as he was only a couple of years or so older than I was, but had to hold my mouth back from smiling at him at the same time. I needed all the support I could get.

"I believe her as well," Alex said. I thought he would. Even though we'd had a rough start, he was the one who had taken care of me the most.

Isaac, however, was clearly going to be the one who was going to get the final say.

"We need to talk this over," he said. "It was only twenty-four hours ago that she was slashing at me with a razorblade and throwing herself through a broken window." He held up his bandaged arm as Exhibit A, and I tried not to experience a twang of guilt upon seeing it. None of this was my fault. These men had kidnapped me at gunpoint. Of course I was going to do everything I could to get away.

"Things are different now," I said. "I didn't believe you yesterday. I didn't know who to trust, if I could even trust anyone. But now I know you were telling the truth about the agents who picked me up wanting to hurt me. Everything has changed. I'm on your side."

"Give her a chance, Isaac," Clay called.

Lorcan nodded. "Yeah, give her a chance."

I held my breath, hoping and praying. I was still in shock after learning the truth about Hollan, but I also wanted to get out of the cellar.

"We still haven't got the code," Isaac pointed out.

I looked at him, my eyes wide, trying to convey my sincerity. "I'm doing everything I can to try to remember."

Kingsley spoke up. "If she's feeling comfortable, she's more likely to allow the memories to come to her."

"See," I said to Isaac, "I'll be more likely to remember the code if you let me out of here. I can help you. I *want* to help you. You just have to let me."

What would they do with me after they got the code? I remembered how I'd told myself there would be nothing to stop them from killing me, but they'd told me they'd taken me to save my life, and now that I'd remembered seeing Hollan after my father had been killed, there was no reason for me not to believe them.

Isaac fixed me with his cool green gaze. I held his stare, determined not to let him intimidate me. His head tilted slightly to the right and he gave a slow nod. "Okay. But you won't leave the house. The doors and windows are locked, and the one you broke has been boarded up. If you try anything, you'll end up down here again, and it will be absolutely the last chance you get. Is that understood?"

I sat on my hands to prevent myself throwing my arms around him in relief. I didn't think Isaac was the hugging type. Instead, I bounced up and down on my hands and looked over to the others, who all appeared equally relieved. Maybe they hadn't been overly comfortable with keeping a young woman locked down in a cellar either.

My pulse quickened in anticipation of being able to see the rest of the house. And sunlight! I'd missed sunlight more than anything, and being able to know the exact time. Though my inner body clock was far better than most, it wasn't perfect, and the total absence of natural daylight had made knowing the time difficult. Combining that with my synesthesia had completely thrown how my brain worked.

I got to my feet, excitement tippy-tapping little feet across my chest. I felt stupidly nervous, for some reason. Alex brushed past me to lead the way, Lorcan right after him. Clay stayed beside me, and he reached out, his hand slipping around my waist to give me a quick squeeze, almost imperceptible, before letting me go. It was enough to tell me he was pleased I was being released.

Kingsley and Isaac remained behind me.

"Right this way," Alex said, as he mounted the stairs and glanced back at me, "but then, you already know that." There was a teasing in his tone, and blood rose to my face. He was referring to my little escape attempt, but other than the cellar, I'd only seen the hallway and the kitchen at the back of the house.

I followed the guys up the stairs, through the door, and out into the hallway.

"Don't get any ideas," Isaac warned from behind my shoulder.

I twisted to see him coming up the stairs behind me, Kingsley behind him. "I won't. I already told you, I'm on your side. I want the code and to find Hollan as much as you guys do. He killed my father and pretended to be our friend. I've got more invested in this than any of you."

I saw them exchange a glance and wondered what it meant. They must know what was on the flash drive. What was on it that was so important? Something they wanted to get their hands on. Something they didn't want Hollan and his team to have access to. Why didn't they want me to know either? What would I be able to do with it? We might be edging toward a kind of tentative trust, but we weren't there yet.

"Y'already know where the kitchen is," said Clay, giving me a grin and shoving his hand through his jaw length locks. He looked to Isaac. "Can I show Darcy the rest of the house?"

Isaac nodded. "Yeah. I've got work to do, anyway."

"I'll show her the office first, then, so we don't disturb you."

Isaac already looked as though this whole thing was boring him. "Whatever you want."

"I've got something to get on with, too," Kingsley said. "Darcy needs to have another break before we try again."

It seemed everyone had something else they needed to be doing, as the others all drifted away, leaving me alone with Clay.

Clay hooked an arm around my neck. "Looks like it's just you and me, sweetheart."

I ducked out from under him. "I'm no one's sweetheart."

He winked at me. "We'll see about that." But he didn't try to put his arm around me again. "We'll start at the back of the house, which you've already seen. The kitchen runs along the rear of the property, and looks out onto the garden."

"I don't even know where we are. I mean, I know we're at least a few hours away from D.C., but I have no idea where."

Clay's lips twisted. "I don't think Isaac would be too happy if I gave any more information away. You know what he's like."

"I guess I'll ask him myself."

"Sure, you do that."

We walked past a couple of closed doors. "That's a downstairs cloakroom," he said, "and a closet. Not too exciting." We'd turned back around, to go past the cellar and head toward the front of the house. "You're already familiar with the cellar."

I rolled my eyes. I didn't want to go down there again, if I could avoid it, even to collect something.

Clay continued, "At the front of the house is the main living room, and there's a den next door, and an office next to that." He lowered his voice. "That's where you can find Isaac most of the time. The rest of us tend to hang out in the den."

I grinned. "Sure."

We reached the bottom of the staircase. "After you," he said.

I mounted the stairs, aware of Clay following, his face aligned directly with my ass. Reaching the top, I found myself on a large landing. A hallway ran in both directions, with numerous white painted doors leading off it.

"How many bedrooms does this place have?" I asked.

"Five." He shot me a grin as I did the numbers. "Don't worry, I'll let you bunk up with me."

"I'll pass, but thanks." I did wonder where I was going to sleep, though. I wasn't going to go back down in the cellar, even if there was a spare bed down there, and they didn't lock the door.

"There's a second office on this floor, too. It's where someone else can work from if the downstairs office is already occupied."

It occurred to me that I might be able to get access to the internet and phones. "Hey, can I call home? My Aunt Sarah will be worried sick about me. I won't tell her where we are—I don't even know, myself—but can I just let her know that I'm safe?"

"I'm not sure. It might be better if she thinks you're dead."

My mouth dropped open. "How can you say that?"

"If everyone thinks you're dead, no one will try to get to her to find out where you are."

Fear clutched at my heart. "You think Hollan might do that?"

"Yeah, if he thinks she knows something."

Panic filled me. "We need to go and get her! I can't leave her out there, unprotected, thinking the worst has happened to me, when she could be in danger herself. She doesn't know what Hollan did. That guy used to come to our house to hang out. What if he tries to slide back into her life again?"

"Take a breath, sugar. If your Aunt Sarah doesn't know anything, she's safe."

I shook my head. "No, I have to warn her."

In my head, I imagined Hollan sitting beside her on the couch, his arm around her shoulders as she sobbed against him.

The digits of her phone number flashed up in front of my eyes, some numbers farther away in my vision, others closer. But I knew it by heart, and that was the main thing. I didn't care what Clay said, or the warnings Isaac had given me about not trying anything. The moment I got to a phone, I planned on calling and warning her about Hollan.

I couldn't shake the thought of him being in my house out of my head. My fury and hatred toward the man grew, and I knew I couldn't let him get away with what he'd done. The son of a bitch pretended to be someone we could trust, when he was actually the complete opposite. My shaking had returned, but I had nowhere to release my pent-up fury.

Clay must have noticed. He took me by both shoulders and ducked his head to look into my eyes. "We ain't gonna let this shithead get away with what he's done. I promise you."

I stared back at him and swallowed hard. There were only inches between our faces, and I was suddenly completely aware of how we were alone. The others had vanished to do their own thing, leaving us to it.

Clay's hand left my shoulder to move up to my face, and he touched the backs of his knuckles against my jaw. "I meant to say sorry to you for dragging you back down the stairs like that the other day."

I closed my eyes briefly and shook my head. "You did what you had to."

"Yeah, but it doesn't mean I'm happy about it."

I lifted my gaze to his again. The air buzzed between us, and I was conscious of how the hand on my shoulder had slipped toward my neck, so he now stood with his fingers against my jaw and the other hand brushing the side of my throat. My breath caught, my heart hammering. I felt my body react to having Clay this close, that fizz of excitement that caused my nipples to tighten and a rush of heat to flood down between my thighs. Clay was sexy in that roguish, long-haired, stubbly kind of way. I didn't think there were many women out there who wouldn't react to being in such close proximity to him. My lips tingled as blood rushed to them, and I couldn't help my gaze slipping down to his mouth as well.

It seemed that was all the encouragement Clay needed. His hand glided from the side of my throat to knot in my hair then his mouth crushed down on mine, stealing the breath from my lungs. My body bowed against his, and my hands moved of their own accord up his back, tracing the solid blocks of muscle beneath his t-shirt.

Desire pulsed through me and our tongues tangled. I knew we had to stop, but I couldn't bring myself to push him away. Instead, I found myself reaching down, wanting to feel the hardness I knew would be waiting for me. My hand closed over the front of his jeans, massaging the ridge of him, and he gasped into my mouth. As though I'd given him the green light, his hand pushed up my t-shirt and dug into the cup of the too-large bra I wore to squeeze my breast. My nipple pebbled at his touch, sparks shooting directly down to my core.

What would the others think of me if they saw me making out with Clay? I'd already kissed Lorcan, but it wasn't like we had any kind of relationship, or that any one of them had more of a claim on me than the other. They'd all been involved in taking me.

I broke the kiss, breathing hard, but Clay didn't step away. Instead, he lowered his head and pressed his forehead to mine.

"Fuck, sugar. I want you so bad."

I shook my head. "We can't. It's not right."

"To hell with that. Who gets to say what is and isn't right?"

I thought that person was probably Isaac, but I wasn't about to go and ask his permission to make out with Clay.

I made myself step away. "We've got more important things to think about."

"There's something more important than sex?" That cheeky twinkle was back in his gray eyes.

"Yes! And no one has even mentioned sex."

"I just did," he pointed out.

I reached out and slapped him on the shoulder. "Well, quit it."

He chuckled. "Do you want to continue the tour, then?"

"Yes! You distracted me."

"So I did."

Someone cleared their throat behind us, that unmistakable sound of a person trying to get noticed, and Clay and I leapt apart as though we were both on fire.

Turning in the direction of the sound, I saw Alex standing at the top of the stairs.

"Hey," I flustered. "We were just discussing sleeping arrangements."

I realized what I'd said and had to stop myself smacking my palm against my forehead. What the hell had I said that for?

"You can have my room," said Alex. "I'm going to assume you don't want to go back down in the cellar."

I shook my head. "No chance."

"You can take my bed, then." He looked to Clay. "Mind if I borrow Darcy?"

"Be my guest," said Clay.

Clay smirked at me, and I narrowed my eyes in return, hoping he wouldn't say anything. I didn't know how much Alex had seen, but for some reason, I cared what Alex thought of me. My lips felt swollen and tingled from all the kissing, and I felt sure it was obvious.

Alex took me by the elbow and led me down the hallway to the end bedroom.

"This one is mine," he told me, pushing open the door. "Isaac has the one at the other end of the house, and the other guys have the rooms in between."

The room was beautiful. A king-sized bed with white cotton sheets. Plush carpets beneath my bare feet. I rushed over to the window on the far side, gazing out across miles of uninterrupted countryside. "The view is incredible."

It had felt like a long time since I'd had space around me, and I wished I could throw myself out of the window and run through the fields with my arms spread wide and my face turned up to the sun. But even though I'd been let out of the cellar, I was still a prisoner here. The men wouldn't allow me to leave. They wouldn't even allow me to make a phone call, though I was determined to contact Aunt Sarah just as soon as I could. The thought of Hollan being anywhere near her, while she remained in the dark, felt like a bug crawling under my skin.

I looked around to find Alex leaning against the frame of the open doorway, his arms crossed over his chest, one foot folded over the other. The side of his mouth was turned up as he watched me.

"This is amazing," I said. "I can't ask you to give up this and sleep down in the cellar."

"Sure you can. We made you sleep down there. Think of this as me getting my comeuppance."

"Together with that kick in the face I gave you," I pointed out.

"Yeah, that as well." He unconsciously rubbed at the bridge of his nose and then lifted his eyes back to mine, blue and piercing, but putting on a mock puppy-dog look. He really was the epitome of devilishly handsome, with his smart shirt rolled up at the sleeves and his blond hair swept back from his face. Where Alex was also blond, Clay was a dirty blond, with the scruffy beard and the stormy grey eyes. Alex was a far more presentable kind of guy. The kind of guy you'd happily take home to your parents, despite the whole kidnapping and shooting thing.

And I was going to be sleeping in his bed.

Chapter Twenty

Alex left me to get settled, but it felt weird being in the room on my own, and I didn't know what to do with myself. There was an adjoining bathroom, and I was relieved to see a bookcase filled with recent releases, which, in normal circumstances, I would have devoured, but I didn't like just hanging around. Aunt Sarah preyed on my mind, and I kept going over all the time Hollan had been to the house and acted like he was my father's friend. I couldn't let it drop, and my anger at the whole situation built up in my chest like an unexploded hydrogen bomb. I felt like we should be doing something, and sitting around in some huge house in the middle of nowhere definitely didn't feel like we were doing anything.

I got to my feet, intending to find Isaac and ask him what he had planned next. Despite having seen Hollan during my hypnosis, we still hadn't extricated the code from my head, and I wanted to know what the plan was afterward. The guys might want the code, but I wanted Hollan dead.

Leaving the room, I headed down the stairs, wondering which of the men I'd bump into first. Would it be weird when I saw Clay again? I didn't want him thinking we were some kind of couple. It had been another moment of madness—a thoroughly enjoyable moment of madness—but I couldn't go around kissing all the guys. What would they think of me?

The scent of food cooking, however, managed to distract me. I hadn't eaten much over the last few days, and my stomach growled.

I walked into the kitchen to find the guys cooking. No, not all of them. Isaac was missing. Doing something important in the office, I guessed.

"There she is." Kingsley was sitting at the kitchen table and spotted me first. Lorcan sat opposite him, looking at something on his cell phone, and I had to fight the urge to snatch it out of his hand. Alex stood at the counter, chopping salad on a board. It was a strangely domesticated setting, and it dawned on me how natural all these men appeared, as though they'd lived together for years and all knew their role, rather than a group who'd been brought together for other reasons.

Clay was standing over the stove, stirring something. It was funny to see this tough guy tending a pot of sauce as though it was a newborn baby. He glanced over his shoulder at me then jerked his head toward the stove. "You wanna taste?"

I stepped toward him. "What is it?"

"The best thing you'll ever put in your mouth, darlin.'"

Was that supposed to be his way of flirting with me? I had to suppress a smile. "Is that right?"

As much as I hated to admit it, I kind of liked Clay.

Reaching his side, I came to a halt. The scents of coconut and lime made my mouth water, and I leaned in to get a better look. "Curry?"

"Green Thai curry. You like it hot?"

I laughed. "As long as I don't regret it the next day."

He dipped the wooden spoon back into the pan and pulled out some sauce, blew on it, then offered me a taste. I opened my mouth, leaning forward, and tentatively poking out my tongue. The sauce was delicious—lemon grass, lime, coconut, and with just the right amount of heat.

"That's amazing."

He grinned. "I aim to please."

"Is there anything I can do to help?"

"Nah. Take a seat and it'll be ready in five."

Sliding onto one of the chairs around the kitchen table, I suddenly felt shy. Lorcan was still engrossed in whatever he was doing, and so it was just me and Kingsley.

"Where's Isaac?" I asked, trying to make conversation. It felt weird hanging out with them when they were technically still my kidnappers.

"Making some calls. We're trying to keep track of Hollan, but it seems he's gone off grid."

"Dammit." I chewed at my lower lip. "Is there anything that can be done to warn my aunt? She's at the house and on her own. I'd hate for him to try something."

Kingsley nodded. "I'll see what we can do."

"Maybe we could bring her here?" I said, my tone rising with hope.

He shook his head. "Not a good idea, Darcy. The less she knows the better."

My lips twisted. Clay had said the same sort of thing.

Thinking of Clay conjured him, and he set down huge bowls of green Thai curry and steaming sticky rice in front of us.

Isaac appeared, but instead of sitting with us, he dished up his food and took it back to the office with him. He barely glanced at me, and I guessed he still wasn't happy about being outvoted about me being allowed out of the cellar.

There were also vegetable spring rolls and dumplings, served with a little bowl of dipping sauce. Alex added the dish of salad, and we were each given bowls and a spoon.

I looked down at the spoon. "No knife and fork?"

"You can always use chopsticks," Alex suggested.

"For curry?"

He laughed. "You might want to use a spoon for the curry, but you can eat the spring rolls with the chopsticks."

Little paper packets of wooden sticks had been provided with the meal. I slipped mine out of the paper, and snapped them down the center to create two separate sticks. At that point, I was stuck.

"I don't know how to use chopsticks," I admitted, feeling uncultured and inadequate. The rest of the guys had already started using theirs, digging into the delicious meal provided.

"I'll show you." Alex reached across the table, and took hold of my right hand. He paused. "You are right handed, aren't you?" I nodded. "Okay," he continued. "You need to hold the top chopstick as though you're holding a pencil. Then put the second chopstick against your ring finger, and hold it with your thumb."

He positioned the chopsticks the way I was supposed to hold them, then looked into my face, his blue eyes bright. "Got it?"

I gave an experimental pinching movement with my hand, and the sticks moved accordingly. "Yeah, I think so," I said, nodding.

Leaning across the table, I used the chopsticks to pick up a spring roll, and dropped it immediately. I had to resist the urge to stab the crispy little cylinder with the stick instead. I was hungry, and I wanted to eat. Casting my gaze around the table, I saw all the guys managing to eat perfectly well with the chopsticks. Damn.

Trying again, I managed to pick up a dumpling.

"Look, I've got it!" I cried in delight, before moving it toward my mouth. I snapped my teeth toward the soft parcel just before it was about to fall, half the dumpling smacking, hot and wet, against my chin. Abandoning the sticks, I used my fingers to prevent the dumpling falling the rest of the way and shoved the remainder into my mouth. I looked up to see Clay watching, a smirk on his face.

"You have such lady-like table manners," he said. "Anyone ever tell you that?"

I managed to finish my mouthful then stuck my tongue out at him.

Too hungry to mess around with chopsticks any longer, I gave them up in favor of the spoon and dug into the curry. It was delicious—the chicken tender, the rice salty. Silence fell around the table as everyone ate—well as silent as it could be with a number of people eating at the same time.

I scraped the bowl clean with the spoon then sat back with a contented sigh, my hands folded across my full stomach.

"That was amazing. Thank you, Clay."

Clay nodded. "Alex helped, too."

"Well, thank you both." I got to my feet, reaching to collect dishes from the others so I could do my part and help clear up, but my hand clashed with someone else. I looked up to find Lorcan and I had both reached for the same dish. We locked eyes, and he gave me a fraction of a nod of acknowledgement. Sparks jumped between us. He was moody and sullen, but the dark hair and tattoos made him sexy as hell.

"Sit down," he told me. "I've got this."

"I want to help," I protested.

His lips tightened. "It's my job. House rules."

Not wanting to step on anyone else's territory, I lowered my backside back down.

Kingsley twisted in his seat to face me. "I know you're probably not feeling like it right now, but we need to get back in your head. It's good you remembered seeing Hollan, but we still need that code."

"Yeah, I know. I'm not backing out."

I debated telling him about my synesthesia, about how I'd be able to see the numbers as soon as I remembered them, would visualize them lit up in front of my eyes like landing lights for an airplane at night, but I held back. It wouldn't make any difference to them how I remembered or saw them. All they wanted was the code, and then they would find Hollan. They would get the flash drive, but I wanted my father's murderer dead, and I wanted to be the one to do it. The guys would never let me tag along, though, I was sure. My only currency was that damned code, and if they got it from me, I'd be left with nothing.

I had to fight with what I had. I couldn't just roll over and let them tell me what was going to happen. I had played a bigger part in this than any of them, and my father had entrusted me with that code with his dying breath.

But had he told me because he wanted me to pass it on to people I could trust, or was it because he wanted me to know what was on that drive?

Isaac returned and slid his used dish into the kitchen sink. He finally turned his attention to me, doing that little head tilt I'd come to recognize in him. "Feeling better now you're out of the cellar?"

I nodded. "Much." I resisted adding, 'no thanks to you.'

Kingsley spoke. "I was just telling Darcy that we still have a job to get on with."

"And I agreed," I said. "I want to see this done as much as you do."

Isaac jerked his head toward the door he'd just walked through. "Okay, let's go through to the living room. We'll all be more comfortable in there."

Lorcan shoved the final dishes into the dishwasher and wiped his hands on the seats of his jeans. The others got up from the table. Isaac led the way, and we all filed toward the front of the house and the living room I hadn't yet been into properly.

The room was decorated like a stage home instead of a house five men lived in. The couches were designed for how they looked instead of comfort, overstuffed with high backs and a slippery satin material. A thick cream rug covered most of the wooden floor, with a dark wood coffee table positioned in the center.

I didn't want to perch on the end of the couch, so I gestured at the coffee table instead. "Think we can move that?"

Alex and Lorcan exchanged a glance then each grabbed an end and hauled it over toward the wall. I sank down onto the rug where the table had been and sat cross-legged. That was better. I could relax like this.

Taking my cue, Kingsley assumed position by sitting opposite me on the floor. Isaac sat on a single chair to the left of Kingsley, and Alex and Lorcan took the uncomfortable looking couch. Clay hung out by the door. He always had a way of acting like he was never truly committing to staying in one spot, like he was always preparing himself for an exit route.

"You remember how it goes?" Kingsley rested his calm gaze on me.

I nodded, but I looked to the others, settling on Isaac. "Before we get started, I've got some questions."

Isaac's lips twisted, and a muscle beside his left eye twitched. "What kind of questions?"

"Who are you guys? You're not government, are you?"

I'd spent enough time with government men during my life to know what they talked and acted like, and it definitely wasn't like these guys.

Isaac shook his head. "No, we're not government. I guess you'd say we're an independent group."

"Just you five?"

"No, there are lots more, but we're the team put together for this."

"For this? Do you mean grabbing me, or retrieving the drive?"

"Both."

On a roll, I continued with the questions. "Who put you together?"

"Think of them like an independent watchdog. There's nothing stopping a government or men in power from becoming corrupt. Hell, there's nothing stopping an entire government from becoming corrupt—we've seen it happen time and time again in other countries. We're here to put an end to things before they can get started."

I frowned, trying to put all the pieces of what he was telling me together in my mind. "So, what, were you like ... headhunted? Did you guys train in particular skills and then were approached to form some kind of tactical team?"

Isaac gave a cold laugh. "Not exactly. We were raised for this."

"Sorry?" I didn't understand.

"You don't know much about our pasts yet, do you, Darcy?"

I shook my head. "No, that's why I'm asking. I want to know more about you."

Isaac's gaze spanned across the other four men in the room. "All of us are orphans, though we weren't the kind of cute baby orphans who people are fighting to adopt. We each lost our parents when we were older children, all over the age of five."

"I'm so sorry," I interrupted, hating to think of any of them—even Isaac—alone and unloved as children.

Isaac continued. "No one wants older boys, especially not older boys who've lost their parents and clearly have issues."

I tried to piece together how them being orphans was connected to what they were doing now. "So, did you know each other as children?"

"Not small children, no, but we were brought together later."

I frowned. "By who?"

"By the same group we work for now. As soon as we started showing talent for something, we were taken away from our respective foster care homes."

"Taken where?"

"To another foster home, of sorts, but this one was run by the people we work for now. Whatever we'd showed natural skills in became our main focus, so from a very early age, we were all learning to become specialists in our fields."

"But you were just kids. How old were you when you were taken?"

Isaac shrugged. "I was the oldest out of the group, and I was almost ten."

Something occurred to me. "But your accent. How could you have been brought up here?"

"My parents moved over here so my father could work for some science company, though I couldn't tell you which one now. Both he and my mother were killed in a car accident during an evening out when I'd been left with a sitter. I didn't have any family back in England, so

I guess no one really knew what to do with me. I ended up in a foster care home here, but I never really lost the accent."

I looked to the others.

"I was the youngest at five," Clay said.

Lorcan raised a hand. "I was seven."

"So was I," Alex said.

"I was older as well," said Kingsley. "I was nine when I was brought to the home."

"So you guys were brought together in a care home and trained?" I looked around each of them, and Kingsley nodded.

"Exactly. And then when we were old enough, we started to be assigned missions. You being the latest."

"Me? I was a mission?"

"Yes, because you revealed what your father had said to you in your final moments."

A pang of regret swelled inside my chest like a balloon. If only I'd not spoken to the reporter, none of this would be happening now. But then the balloon popped. If I hadn't spoken to the press, I wouldn't know who my father's killer had been. I would be continuing to daydream my way through my life, with no focus. And as mixed as my feelings were toward the men I sat in the room with now, I also didn't want to go back to a life where they weren't in it.

"What about the memory stick?" I said eventually. "Were any of you given that mission when my father died?" Isaac was talking about preventing corruption before it happened, but then why had my father still had to take the flash drive? Shouldn't one of the team stepped in?

Isaac shook his head. "It was before our time. We were still in training, barely more than kids ourselves. Someone should have been there to help your father, but it wasn't picked up on soon enough. I'm sorry for that."

My face pinched as I tried to process all of this information. "It wasn't your fault. Like you said, you were barely more than kids yourselves." At only a couple of years older than me, Clay would only have been sixteen, Alex and Lorcan would have just turned eighteen. Kingsley and Isaac might have been a little older, but not old enough to deal with whatever corruption was going on in the FBI.

"Even so, someone should have stopped it before it got so out of hand. Your father should never have needed to take the memory stick."

"So he did the right thing?" A tight, painful pinching closed my throat. My instincts had always told me my father had been a good man, and he wouldn't have taken something confidential if he hadn't absolutely had to, but when the press picked up on it, and everyone was talking about how he had betrayed his country by doing so, it was hard not to hear those things. Even Agent Fucking Hollan's absence after the funeral had made me wonder if everyone else was right and my father had done a bad thing. People said he'd stolen the information in return for money, and the people who had shot him must have been involved in the deal. The deal had simply gone bad, and my father had paid for his part in it. I'd never wanted to listen to those things, but it was hard not to after awhile. Having his innocence laid out in front of me now felt like a baptism. I could think of my dad in a good light again, without the fear that he'd never been the man I'd loved my whole life.

"So he took the memory stick to try to keep it out of the hands of the wrong people?"

Isaac nodded. "That's about the sum of it."

I needed to know what was on that stick.

I'd seen these men as the enemies, but now how I felt toward them had changed. I'd been so wrapped up in myself, and my father's death, I hadn't given any thought to the guys and what they might have been through during their lives. They were all orphans, having lost their parents at a young age. I wondered if the place where they'd been brought to train as young children had anything akin to a parental figure, or if it had been hard and cold. Had they had a mother-figure to sing them to sleep at night, or place a cool towel against their foreheads when they were sick? Or had they only had each other?

My heart broke at the thought of any of them as young children, having lost both parents and picked out by whomever it was they worked for to train as this special taskforce. Isaac was the prickliest out of them all, but I tried to imagine how it had been for him, moving to a strange country, only to lose both of his parents and end up in a foster home with no friends or family to speak of. No wonder he was a cold fish.

I was about to talk myself into trying to be nicer to him, when I reminded myself that they had kidnapped me and locked me in a cellar for several days. I had every right to still be pissed at him, or any of them, for that matter.

Isaac lifted his eyebrows. "Any more questions, Darcy, or can we get started now?"

"We can get started."

Familiar nerves fluttered in my stomach, and I swallowed hard, trying to push them back down. Revisiting my father's death was traumatic, and it wasn't something I wanted to do. Maybe that was what all the questions had been about—my attempt at delaying the inevitable. But if I was going to remember the number, I had to keep going. It would have been what my father wanted.

"Remember that it's the words your father says to you which you need to focus on," Kingsley said. "Try not to be distracted by everything else."

"By the man who murdered him, you mean?"

"Yeah, and try not to panic again. You're just an observer. It's not really happening."

We went through the same routine, me sitting with my eyes closed, breathing how he instructed, and picturing a movie theatre screen in front of me. Even before I'd seen anything, my heartrate increased. It wasn't a fun thing, to witness your father's death over and over, but I knew I needed to get those numbers.

The screen flickered. There I was, standing with my back facing outward, shouting at my poor dad. He had his back to the window, his face pinched with his own frustration at his teenage daughter. I couldn't help my attention being drawn back toward the black glass, watching for the flash of movement. Hollan must have shot my dad, and then slipped in through the kitchen door, which was how I'd seen his reflection in the glass. Had he searched the house for the flash drive while I'd been on the floor with my dad bleeding out, screaming for help? He must have heard me. If he'd listened harder, he'd have been the one who'd heard that code instead of me. Things would have been so different if he had. Hollan would have gotten hold of the drive and been able to access whatever was on it. Whatever my dad had been trying to hide from Hollan and his team would have landed directly in their hands.

In the landscape of my memory, I heard gunshots, and my dad fell forward.

Suddenly, I was back in the memory again. One moment, I'd been in the chair, watching, the next I sat on the floor of the living room with my father in my arms. Blood seeped through to my skin and clothing, but I bit down on the horror and panic surging up inside me and threatening to take control. The words that had filled my mind on that day tried to crowd my thoughts—*don't die, don't die, don't die*—but I forced them away. I needed to focus on my dad and what he was saying to me. I couldn't think about the man I knew was rummaging through our house to find the item he'd killed my father for.

Instead, I looked down into my dad's face. The man who had raised me. Tears poured down my cheeks, and somehow I knew I was crying in the real world as well. I placed my palm against his cheek, wanting so desperately to make things better and knowing it was impossible. I wanted to look into his blue eyes, eyes so like mine, and try to give him some comfort, but it didn't matter what I did now, the outcome would always be the same. This was the father of my memories. It wasn't really him, but that didn't make things any easier.

I moved my gaze down to his mouth, trying hard to ignore the sticky hot blood seeping against my skin. *Concentrate, concentrate, concentrate.* Everything around me threatened to draw my attention away. Knowing Hollan was somewhere in the house with us made me want to hunt him down and make him pay, but I had to stay focused. I had to remember. The numbers were already in my head somewhere, I just needed to open up the pathway that would take them from my stored long term memory to my active memory.

Staring down into my father's face, I watch his lips move. A bubble of blood swelled like oil between them, and I flinched as it burst, spattering specks of red across his chin. I held back a sob. I wanted to look away, but I couldn't. This was too important. I blinked back my tears, needing to see, and watch as his lips formed the words. As my father spoke the final words I'd ever hear him say, the numbers appeared before me in boxes. Each digit took its own position in the space around me.

I had the code.

Chapter Twenty-one

With a gasp, my eyes shot open and I found myself back in the living room, sitting cross-legged on the plush cream rug. My face was damp, the taste of salt clinging to my lips as though I'd spent time caught in ocean spray. My heart thundered in my chest, and I fought to slow its pace.

Kingsley leaned forward, frowning at me in concern. I wanted him to move back. He inhabited the space where my synesthesia allowed me to see the code my father had given me, the numbers hanging in the air in front of me. But the guys still didn't know about that.

At least now I could visualize the numbers, I knew I'd never forget them. Kingsley had been right when he said my mind had absorbed the information on a subconscious level and stored it away in my long term memory. I had accessed the code now, and I wasn't going to let it go anywhere.

The men all stared at me.

"Well?" Isaac was the first to speak. "What do you remember?"

I shook my head. "I'm sorry. It was all too much again. It was just the blood and him dying. I couldn't concentrate on anything else."

Isaac slammed his fist down on the armrest of the chair and jumped to his feet. "Bloody hell!"

"I'm sorry." I allowed my face to crumple, my lower lip quivering as I remembered the emotions I'd experienced in recalling my father's murder. "Maybe I'm just tired. I've been through a lot, and today has been crazy. It's been an overload of information."

Kingsley looked at me in sympathy then turned to Isaac. "She's right. We can't ask the brain to pull up buried memories when it's already exhausted."

A twinge of guilt plucked at my gut for lying to them.

A part of me wanted to tell them the number, if only to offload, to put its burden and the weight it carried onto their shoulders. But the code was my only leverage. If I gave them the number, what reason would they have to keep me around? I needed to get to Hollan, and right now these men were the only connection I had to him.

Now I had the number, I needed time to think. The excuse of needing some rest would buy me that time, and I'd figure out what to do afterward.

"Maybe if we got the memory stick first, it would be easier for me to remember," I suggested cautiously. I didn't want to make them suspicious of me. "Give me something to focus on. You said all sorts of things can trigger a memory—smells, sounds, tastes—so why not actually being able to hold the one thing that makes this all so important?"

"Did you ever see it yourself?" Kingsley asked.

I shook my head. "No. Why?"

"If it's not in your memory already, linked to your memory of your father that night, then it won't do anything to help."

"But I've made that connection now," I pressed. "I'm sure it will help to get the drive first."

"It's not that simple." Isaac paced across the room with his hands shoved in the pockets of his suit pants, his head down. "Getting it back will literally be a military operation."

"You know where it is, then?"

"Hollan will know."

"So you know where *he* is?" I prompted, trying to squeeze them for every detail.

"We know how to find him."

Damn, he was being vague. Not that I thought I'd be able to take on Hollan by myself, but right now if I could get hold of a gun and that son of a bitch was standing right in front of me, I wouldn't hesitate in making him pay for what he did.

The thing worrying me the most was if I gave them the code, they would leave me behind, or worse. My use would have been served.

"That's enough for now." Alex got to his feet. "It's probably time we all got some rest."

I didn't like the idea of wasting time sleeping, but though I'd been pretending to be too tired to remember, exhaustion suddenly weighed down on my limbs, and I found myself hiding a yawn behind my hand. The thought of Alex's big bed, with the soft white sheets and the heavy feather duvet made me long to crawl beneath the covers and snuggle my face into the pillow. I'd been sleeping on the floor for the past few nights, which perhaps was a little stupid on my part, but it had felt like the right thing to do at the time.

Alex stopped in front of me and offered me his hand. I smiled up at him gratefully and took it, his palm soft and warm, and he pulled me to my feet.

"'Night," the others called to me, and I raised a hand to wave them goodbye.

I caught Isaac's eye and a chill went through me. He didn't smile or say goodnight. I wanted to think he was just being his usual asshole self, but there was part of me—the guilty part, perhaps—that wondered if he knew I'd lied.

We reached the stairs and Alex paused. "I'll bring you up some of the clothes from the cellar so you can find something to sleep in, or change into in the morning. You're welcome to borrow one of my t-shirts, or anything else you want. Help yourself to whatever is in the drawers."

I gave him a grateful smile. "Thanks, Alex."

He left me to go back down to the cellar. I didn't plan on ever stepping foot in that place again.

I trotted back up the stairs and went into the bedroom. The bed was as big and fluffy as I'd remembered, and I smoothed my hand across the top of the soft sheets, before heading into the bathroom.

Damn. I didn't have a toothbrush.

A gentle knock came at the bedroom door, and I poked my head out of the bathroom to see Alex ducking through.

"You don't have to knock on your own bedroom door," I told him as he entered, his arms bundled with things.

"You might have been getting changed."

I hadn't had the chance to figure out what I was wearing to bed yet, but the thought of one of his big t-shirts did sound comfortable.

He dumped the pile of clothes down on the bed, and I noticed a couple of pairs of panties and a bra dangling out of the pile. The sight of them embarrassed me, and they weren't even mine, not really. I wondered which of the guys had gone out of their way to purchase women's clothes and underwear, or if it was possible one or more of them had a girlfriend or even wife hidden away somewhere.

"Thanks," I told him, picking up each item and stashing it away on the occasional chair in the corner. "I really appreciate it." My toothbrush fell out of the bundle, and I bent to pick it up. "And extra thanks for this!"

"I thought you'd need it after that curry."

I laughed. "Are you trying to tell me something?"

Alex went to the dresser and slid open a drawer. He rummaged around and picked out a t-shirt and threw it to me. At about six feet two, Alex was tall and lean, and the t-shirt would hang somewhere mid-thigh on me.

"Thanks. I'll go and change." Without thinking, I brought the material up to my nose and inhaled. It smelled distinctively of Alex, the cotton worn and soft as butter.

I glanced up to catch him watching me, and I snatched the t-shirt away from my face.

Alex's blue eyes lit with pleasure though he controlled his mouth enough not to show it.

"I'll leave you to it," he said.

My teeth snagged my lower lip. "I feel bad you sleeping down in the cellar."

He shrugged. "Well, you shouldn't. We made you sleep down there for three nights."

He had a point.

"Even so," I said. "It seems stupid when this bed is plenty big enough for both of us. You just stick to your side, and I'll stick to mine."

"You have a side now?" he asked, his tone flirtatious.

"Yes! The one closest to the window. And don't try anything. I've got a mean right foot."

He chuckled. "I'm a gentleman."

Only when you want to be, I thought but didn't say. My memories of Alex grabbing my legs in the back seat of Hollan's car remained fresh in my mind. He hadn't been such a gentleman then. Of course, he'd been trying to save my life. I just hadn't known it at the time. I tried not to look too deeply into the reason why thinking of Alex as rough and ready gave me a thrill.

"Okay," he agreed. "As long as you're sure."

"Yeah, I'm sure."

I took the t-shirt and toothbrush back into the bathroom to get ready. When I emerged five minutes later, my legs were bare. Tugging at the hem of Alex's t-shirt, I tried to cover a little more of my thighs.

Hopping beneath the sheets, using them to cover the rest of my body, I snuggled down, facing away from the side Alex would be occupying, toward the window. It was pitch black outside now, only the light from the moon and the stars blinking. We were in the middle of nowhere with no manmade light to ruin the night sky.

I heard the rustle of fabric as he got undressed, and I wondered exactly how much he was planning on wearing to bed ... not that I had any intention of finding out. Alex's weight depressed the mattress on the other side of the bed as he climbed in as well.

There was a little jolt of movement, followed by a click of a light switch, then the room fell into darkness.

I expected to lie awake for ages waiting to sleep, but all my claims of being tired must have been true, because the moment my eyes slipped shut, I was sound asleep.

FEATHER LIGHT TOUCHES drifted down the side of my body to caress my naked thigh. My body woke, though my mind still floated, caught in that wasteland between wake and sleep. Teeth grazed my neck, and I let out a moan, wriggling down in the softness of the warm bed. The light touches became more insistent, and I twisted to meet them to find a strong, hard thigh wedged up between my legs. A hot mouth closed over mine, a tongue tracing my lips. I ground down against the thigh between my legs, my pussy already wet and swollen in response. A hand found my breast beneath the oversized t-shirt I wore, and clever fingers pinched my nipple, rolling and teasing me to a sensitive peak.

I wanted more, but I couldn't quiet bring myself to wake fully. My body plunged onward, seeking its release. It was my sole focus, the only thing I wanted or needed in that moment. I didn't care who the hands, or mouth, or thigh belonged to. I just needed to be sated.

I ground down harder on the thigh between my legs, my arousal escalating fast. A hand slipped into the back of my panties to cup one cheek of my ass. My flesh squeezed and massaged. Fingers grazed my tight hole, and I let out a moan, the sound pressed against the mouth still working mine. The leg moved, and I mourned the loss of pressure, but my underwear was stripped from my thighs, and what I'd been rocking against was replaced by something else.

Still half asleep, I was caught up in a confusion of hands and mouths, only aware of kisses and strokes and a building pressure at my core. I wanted it so badly, reached for it, climbed toward it. I didn't care about anything other than coming.

My orgasm shattered through me, pulse after pulse, narrowing my whole existence down to only this intense pleasure rolling through me. Leaving me gasping for breath, and shuddering with little aftershocks as my orgasm faded away ...

Chapter Twenty-two

I opened my eyes, still breathing hard. What had happened? Had I been dreaming, or was it something more?

I glanced over and, in the dark, made out Alex's sleeping form huddled beneath the sheets. He lay on his side, facing away from me. His breathing came deep and even, and if I'd made any sounds during my sleep, they hadn't disturbed him.

Yet the sheets felt cool and damp with sweat, and I reached out and gently touched the back of his neck. His skin was damp, the blond locks at his nape coiled with moisture, as though he'd been doing something that would have caused him to perspire.

I pressed my thighs together, feeling my own wetness caused by what—the dream, or had it been more? Then I realized something else. I'd gone to sleep in Alex's t-shirt and my panties, but though I was definitely still wearing the t-shirt, a cool draft of air caressed between my thighs.

Damn. Where the hell had my underwear gone? Had I rolled them off in my sleep, or had Alex had something to do with it? Could both of us have been brought together unknowingly?

In a panic, I touched my fingers between my legs and then brought my hand to my nose. I sighed in relief. I only got my own musky tang, and not the distinctive salty scent of semen. So what the hell had happened to my underwear?

Reaching around in the bed, and using my legs and toes to feel around as well, I located the slip of material rolled into a twist. They definitely looked as though they'd been removed during sex, but there was nothing else to show it had been anything more than my overactive imagination. Had I been dry humping Alex in my sleep? God, how embarrassing. Had he noticed and just chosen to ignore me, or had he responded to me, not realizing I'd still been asleep.

The only way to find out for sure would be to ask him directly, and there was no way in hell I planned on doing that. How would that conversation go? 'Hey, Alex, did I try to fuck you in your sleep the other night?' Not. Going. To. Happen.

I felt wide awake now. The house was quiet, and I figured the others were all sleeping, too. An idea occurred to me, and sent a rush of adrenaline through my body, making my heart race and my breath grow shallow. Did I dare attempt it? The guys wouldn't even have to know.

Trying not to make any noise, I slid my legs out of bed, my bare feet making contact with the plush carpet. I got to my feet then froze, casting a glance over my shoulder to make sure Alex hadn't been disturbed. He hadn't.

I moved quickly to the door, opened it as quietly as possible, and slipped out into the hallway. Pausing again, my ears strained for any sign of anyone else being awake. From behind one of the doors, I heard the rhythmical vibrations of someone snoring, and made a mental note not to share a bed with whoever that was.

When Clay had given me the tour earlier, he'd told me one of the upstairs rooms was a second office, but though it was bound to have a phone, I didn't want to risk being heard. The guys were sleeping all around me, and the office downstairs was at the front of the house. They'd never hear me from there.

Would all the doors leading to the outside world be locked? Through the window earlier, I'd spotted a couple of vehicles parked outside, one of which being the car they'd brought me here in. It occurred to me that I could search the house for the keys. If I found them and got out, I could drive myself home. Of course, if I did that, I wouldn't be any closer to finding Hollan or the memory stick, and the guys would never trust me again. Not that they should, anyway.

I tiptoed down the stairs, paranoid for that tell-tale creaky step, and reached the office at the front of the house. My ears strained the whole time, listening for any sign that someone might be awake. The house wasn't old, but it still groaned and creaked, and I froze each time I heard something new, my heart racing.

I reached the office. The door was shut, and I carefully tried the handle. For a moment, I thought it might have been locked, but I twisted the knob a little harder and the door cracked open. Beyond, the room was in darkness, just like the rest of the house. No one was in there.

Not wanting to risk putting on a light, I slipped inside and closed the door softly behind me. Ghostly white light from the moon filtered through the window, allowing me to see where I was going. A large desk had been positioned in the corner of the room, and what I wanted most—a phone—sat beside the computer.

The digits of my home phone number flashed up in front of my face, illuminating in order to show which sequence they went in. I longed to hear my Aunt Sarah's voice, to tell her everything would be okay, and to be careful of Hollan. Clay had told me not to warn her about him, but how could I not?

I crossed the room and came to a halt at the desk. Knowing there would be no turning back once I'd dialed that number, I hesitated, but then I pushed my worries away and picked up the handset. After they'd kept me in a cellar for three days, the least they owed me was a phone call home. Even prisoners were offered that much.

I punched in the number, still shining brightly in the space in front of me.

The phone rang, and I pressed the handset closer to my ear. *Come on, come on.* What if she didn't answer? It was the middle of the night, and she would most likely be asleep. But she knew I was missing. Receiving a phone call in the middle of the night when your niece was missing surely would almost be expected, though I guaranteed she'd be thinking it was bad news.

"Hello?"

I'd assumed she would have been bleary and her voice sleep filled, but instead it was sharp.

"Aunt Sarah. It's me. It's Darcy." The sound of her voice caused unexpected emotion to swell up inside me. My eyes filled with tears, and I clamped my hand to my mouth to hold back a sob. I didn't want her to think I was hurt.

"Oh, my God, Darcy. Is that really you?"

My voice broke, but I managed to get the words out. "It's me, Aunt Sarah."

"Where are you? Are you hurt? Are you safe?"

"I'm okay."

"Where are you?" she asked again, the pitch of her tone higher than I was used to. "Everyone's been searching for you. I've had the police here."

I stiffened. "Only the police?"

"No, the FBI as well. What have you gotten yourself mixed up in, Darcy?"

"It isn't about me. It's about Dad."

"Michael? He's been dead six years. What on earth could he have to do with you vanishing like that?"

"I didn't vanish, Aunt Sarah. I was taken."

Didn't she know about the shooting? Had Hollan somehow covered it up? Had no one made the connection between the FBI turning up at my house and then me going missing?

"Just tell me where you are, Darcy, and I'll come and get you. Or for God's sake, come home. Everyone has been worried sick."

"It's not as—" Above my head, a floorboard creaked. My gaze shot up, staring at the ceiling. Someone was up.

"I'm sorry Aunt Sarah, but I have to go. I just wanted to tell you not to worry about me, okay? I'll try to call again when I can. I love you."

I caught her calling my name as I carefully replaced the handset. More movement came from upstairs. Someone was definitely awake. I had to hope they'd gotten up to use the bathroom and then were going straight back to bed again, but instead I heard the distinctive *thump thump thump* of footsteps crossing a bedroom floor.

Shit.

I moved fast, not wanting to be caught inside the office.

Running for the door, I slipped out into the hallway and pulled the door shut behind me again. I hesitated, unsure what to do next. Should I hide somewhere? Or try to get back into the bedroom with Alex. Whoever had woken might have already gone to check on me and found me gone.

"Darcy?"

My indecision had gotten me caught. I looked up, toward the top of the stairs. A figure was cast in shadows. From the height and build, I knew it was either Lorcan or Isaac.

"What are you doing down there?"

From the accent, I knew it was Isaac, and my stomach dropped. I could have distracted Lorcan, but Isaac was sharper.

"Nothing," I said. "I woke up thirsty, so I was just heading to the kitchen to get a glass of water."

He took a number of steps down toward me. He wore only a t-shirt and the pair of boxers I assumed he must have slept in. "There's a faucet in the bathroom."

I shrugged, holding out my empty hands. "No glass. And I had enough of being forced to stick my head under the faucet to drink when I was down in the cellar."

I'd hoped my jibe might have made him feel bad and get him to back down, but that wasn't how Isaac worked.

"You can't go wandering around the house in the middle of the night. What if one of us mistook you for an intruder and shot you in the dark?"

I blinked at him, feigning innocence. "Sorry. I didn't know. No one told me I wasn't allowed to leave the bedroom."

"Well, I'm telling you now," he said, coolly.

"Fine." My response was equally as frosty. "But can I get that glass of water first, or will you accidentally shoot me in the back?"

He lifted his bandaged arm. "Payback for this," he said, and I couldn't tell if he was kidding or not. Probably not. I hadn't heard Isaac joke about anything yet. Maybe it was the British in him. I'd always heard they had a dry sense of humor.

I didn't reply, but forced myself to hold his gaze to show him he wasn't going to intimidate me. It wasn't easy, especially as I'd been down here doing something I knew he'd be seriously pissed about if he found out, but I forced myself to do it anyway.

"Fine," he said eventually, his arms folded across his chest as he glowered at me. "Go and get your glass of water, then get back to bed. You're supposed to be resting, remember. Can't have that brain of yours being tired, not when we're trying to get important information out of it."

In that moment, I felt a spike of bitter glee for withholding that little bit of information. I wanted to throw it in his face—that I had already remembered, but I wasn't going to tell him yet—but I kept my mouth shut. I'd only be cutting off my own nose, and Isaac wouldn't be happy that I'd kept it from him for as long as I had. When I told them, eventually, I'd do it in a way they'd think I'd only just remembered so it didn't get me in yet more trouble.

I turned from Isaac and went to the kitchen. I felt him shadowing me the whole way. God, why did he have to be such a creep? I went straight to the cupboards, opening the doors until I found the one holding the glassware, and then filled a tall glass with cool water from the faucet. I took a couple of big gulps of water to keep up the pretense of me waking because I'd been thirsty, though actually, by that point and because of the excitement of talking to Sarah and the encounter with Isaac, I actually was thirsty.

He waited for me in the hallway to make sure I went straight back to bed, I assumed. I lifted the glass in a sarcastic salute while I brushed past him,

I sensed him watching me the whole way back to the bedroom and was relieved to be able to shut the door on him. Alex's sleeping form still lay beneath the blankets in almost exactly the same position I'd left him in. Thank God he hadn't woken. I didn't want to have to explain my nocturnal wanderings to anyone else, though I was sure Isaac would fill them all in, come morning.

I set the half-drunk glass of water on the nightstand, careful not to disturb Alex, and then slipped back into bed. My conversation with Aunt Sarah turned over in my mind. I hoped I'd not upset her more by calling her. What did it mean that she hadn't heard about the shootout on the street and that she hadn't known the FBI had been at the house that morning? Had she thought I'd just run off?

Though I hadn't expected to sleep again that night, my waking thoughts turned into dreams, and I drifted off to oblivion.

Chapter Twenty-three

The blare of an alarm sounding through the house burst me from sleep, my heart pounding. Bright sunlight poured through the window, and I squinted in its glare. It was morning, but this was no regular alarm. It sounded more like a smoke alarm, only louder and more insistent.

Something was shoved at me, and I looked around in confusion to see Alex standing beside me. He was pulling on his jeans with one hand, and held a handgun in the other.

"Get dressed," he snapped. "We've got company."

"What?"

"Just do it."

I climbed out of bed to yank on the jeans he'd thrown at me. To my surprise, he leaned over the bed and pressed a point on the large, cushioned headboard. The whole headboard fell toward the bed, and my mouth gaped. Numerous weapons, guns, bullets, and even knives were attached to the wall behind, and I spotted a couple of canisters, though I didn't know what they contained.

Who the hell were these people?

"You know how to shoot?" he asked.

I nodded.

"Take this." He pushed the gun he was holding into my hand. It felt good, the metal warmed from his skin, the weight enough to feel solid without inhibiting my movement. "Only use it if you have to, but try to stay hidden. They'll be here for you."

I didn't think my jaw was capable of hanging open any farther, but apparently it was. "What?"

The bedroom door burst open, and Kingsley stood in the open doorway. He also held a large gun at his side. "We've got to move."

Alex yanked the final assault rifle from the back of the headboard and took a couple of the canisters as well. "Yeah, we're coming."

"Where are the others?" I yelled over the alarm.

Kingsley glanced over his shoulder, as though expecting to see them. "Preparing themselves."

"For what?" I still didn't know what the alarm was for.

"A fight. We've got uninvited guests on the property."

"What, in the house?" I said in fear.

"Not yet, but they will be soon."

"Shit."

Kingsley turned around and ran back out, down the hallway. Alex grabbed me by the elbow and took after him, pulling me along. I just caught a glimpse of Clay already running down the stairs. Where were Lorcan and Isaac? Were they on the ground floor already?

"We need to get her down into the cellar," Kingsley called over his shoulder.

Alex dragged me harder. "Yeah, we're coming."

I pulled back on him, my heart lurching. "No way, I'm not going back down in the cellar."

"Yes, you are. But don't freak out. You're not going alone, and you're not staying down there either."

"What are you talking about?"

From somewhere in the house, gunshots sounded. *Oh, God.* Had someone been shot? I couldn't stand to think of any of the guys being hurt. Even Isaac.

I was caught up in the flurry of movement and panic, Alex's body buffering me forward. Fear sharpened the world around me, the ornate wooden banisters of the staircase we ran toward standing out in sharp contrast to the cream walls beyond. We were running toward the gun-fire, not away from it, but where else could we go? At the top of the house, we were trapped.

We reached the stairs and ran down, Kingsley in front of me, Alex behind.

We'd only gotten halfway down the stairs when, ahead of us, the front door burst open. Somewhere, glass broke with a crash. Men in protective gear piled through the door, but, being at a higher point and seeing them first, we had the advantage. Alex reached out and grabbed me, pulling me back and behind him, to protect me with his body. Automatically, Kingsley dropped to a crouch and pointed his handgun, firing several shots. Behind him, and positioned a couple of steps higher, Alex lifted the rifle so it pointed over the top of Kingsley's head, and let off a spray of gunfire. The first man in the doorway managed to fire a couple of shots, but the barrage of bullets sent him staggering back. The noise was intense, hammering on my eardrums, and I couldn't stop myself from cowering down and covering my ears with my free hand for protection.

"Stay behind me!" Alex yelled.

I had the gun clutched tightly in my hand, but Alex had told me it was only for emergencies. This whole thing felt like one huge emergency to me, but I wasn't about to start firing shots unless I had to. I still hadn't seen either Lorcan or Isaac, and Clay had vanished down the stairs before us. I didn't want to risk accidentally shooting any of them.

More gunshots were fired at the back of the house, toward the kitchen, and my heart twisted, trying not to think who the bullets had been meant for.

"Shit," Kingsley said, "they must be surrounding the house."

How were we going to get out? By shooting our way out of here?

The shapes of two more men appeared through the front door.

Alex worked quickly and threw one of the canisters he'd taken out of the headboard over-arm toward the front door. "Move!" he shouted. "Fast!"

Sudden smoke filled the front of the hall, driving the men back. Alex had thrown it far enough that the thick white smoke didn't affect us for the moment, but that wouldn't last for long. As soon as it drifted this way, we'd be coughing and spluttering just like the men attacking us.

We ran down the remainder of the stairs, staying low. Alex paused at the bottom to cover us with his gun as we turned the corner, heading toward the back of the house, and the rear of the staircase where the door to the cellar was located. I didn't want to go back down there, but I didn't want to end up dead either.

Movement came from the back of the house, and my eyes widened as I saw Lorcan running toward us. His hazel eyes appeared darker with anger, his jaw rigid. A sudden gunshot cracked through the air, and he fell forward, crashing to the floor.

"No!" I screamed.

A man was behind him, armed, and Kingsley didn't hesitate in firing off two shots, bringing the man down as well. The gunman lay face down, not moving, but my attention wasn't on him, it was on Lorcan, who was trying to get back up. Automatically, I reached for Lorcan, but Kingsley held me back.

"Leave him!"

"What? No! He's hurt. He needs help."

I darted for him again. Seeing someone shot right in front of me brought back so many memories of seeing my dad shot, too. I hadn't been able to do anything to help my dad, but I sure as hell wasn't just going to leave Lorcan to die.

Kingsley grabbed me, held me tight, even as I fought against him. "Quit it, Darcy! Alex will help him. You're too important to risk losing."

I choked back a sob. *I* wasn't important. Only what was in my head. Alex pushed past me to help Lorcan.

I didn't know where gunfire would be coming from next. The men at the front of the house were bound to find a way through the smoke, and there were clearly men coming in from the rear of the property, too. I braced myself, expecting to receive a bullet at any moment. Who were these people? Why were they attacking the house?

Alex bent to Lorcan, and Kingsley pulled me past him and turned the corner to the door of the cellar. I didn't want to go back down there, but if it was the choice of facing my fears or being shot, I was tackling them head on.

Kingsley yanked open the door, and then slammed his hand on the switch to light up my ex-prison cell. It looked exactly the same as I had left it—bare mattress and all. I assumed the only difference would be the empty drawers as Alex had brought most of the clothes up to his room for me last night.

"Go!" he told me, giving me a slight shove in the middle of my back.

There wasn't any time to waste. I ran down the stairs as fast as I could without falling over my feet. From the thuds and vibrations on the stairs, Kingsley was right behind me.

I risked glancing over my shoulder to see Alex with his arm around Lorcan, Lorcan's arm slung over Alex's neck as he helped him to follow us. I didn't know if Alex had something pressed against the gunshot wound in Lorcan's back, but I hoped he did. If we were going to hide out in the cellar, Lorcan might bleed to death before we got help. Yes, Alex was medically trained, but if Lorcan needed surgery, there would be nothing he could do from down here.

"Where are Clay and Isaac?" I asked, panicked.

"They're coming," Kingsley said. "They went to deal with our friends. They'll be right behind us."

He went directly around the staircase, to the area I'd used as my little cubby hole, and dragged out all of the blankets, throwing them to one side. What was he doing? He reached to the top and bottom corners of the brickwork and pressed hard. I watched in shocked amazement as the wall I'd spent several nights huddled up against swung inward, revealing a darkened passage behind.

"It's a false wall?"

"Yeah, front of the brick only."

My fear of what was happening overhead was momentarily overshadowed by my disbelief. "What if I'd found it? I might have escaped."

He looked over his shoulder at me. "But you didn't, did you? Now, are we getting out of here?"

"What about the others?"

"They'll follow along behind."

I hated the idea of running when the others might be in trouble. "No, we can't leave them."

More gunshots sounded somewhere in the property, each one making me flinch.

Kingsley's mouth tightened, his nostrils flaring. "We don't have a choice."

I glanced over my shoulder to where Alex was still holding up an injured Lorcan. "Let them go first."

Kingsley shook his head. "No, you'll be faster. Now just fucking move, Darcy!"

It wasn't often I heard Kingsley swear, and the urgency in his tone got me moving. I didn't like the claustrophobia of the dark tunnel, but I had to keep going. It was either that, or I waited here and probably ended up dead.

I had to stay in a crouch, ducking my head so I didn't smack it against the ceiling. There was no light, so I used the hand that wasn't holding the gun to feel my way along. I dreaded the floor suddenly dropping out in front of me, or the ceiling plunging lower so I smacked my head on it in the dark, but it remained uniform.

Scuffs and scrapes behind me signified Kingsley pursuing, followed by scrapes and heavy breathing as Alex helped Lorcan. Lorcan must have been in significant pain, but if he was, he didn't give voice to it. Only the hissing of breath as he sucked air in over his teeth gave any indication he was hurt.

I had no idea where I was going. How long would the tunnel go on, and where would it come out? I was terrified I would emerge somewhere, only to find men on the other side, waiting to put bullets in our heads. I worried that Clay and Isaac wouldn't get out. They must know where we'd gone, however. This was clearly a planned escape route.

I kept going and tried not to think of spiders as cobwebs caught at my face in the dark. Bugs should have been the least of my concern, but I still couldn't stop the shudder wracking through me at the thought of their spindly legs crawling over my skin. The muscles in my back, neck, and thighs ached, my whole body trembling. My lungs burned from the exertion, but I pushed myself forward, knowing if I stopped I would be blocking the tunnel and trapping the guys behind me.

"How much farther?" I gasped, my legs shaking from exertion as much as fear.

"Not far," came Kingsley's deep voice. "Just keep going."

I hated the dark. It had never bothered me before, but this, combined with the time I'd spent in the cellar, was making me wish I lived in one of those countries where the sun never fully went down. The tunnel was pitch black, and my mind kept playing tricks on me, thinking I was about to smack straight into some unseen foe.

But finally there was a change to the depth of the darkness, and I spotted a pinprick of daylight up ahead. I had forgotten it was morning, with bright sunshine. Somehow being stuck in the dark managed to eradicate any concept of what the outside world should be like.

"Nearly there, Darcy," Kingsley encouraged. "You're doing great."

I wanted to turn around and yell at him that I was doing the absolute opposite of great, but instead I gritted my teeth and held back a growl of frustration. After all, I only had to move myself, and I wasn't even hurt, whereas Lorcan still struggled on behind me, despite being shot. This must be much harder for the men. Not only was Lorcan hurt, but they were also far bigger than I was, and must be finding it more difficult to maneuver in the confined space. If they could do it, I definitely could, too.

Focusing on that nugget of determination inside me, I headed toward the light.

Chapter Twenty-four

Getting out of here wasn't going to be straightforward.
As I got closer, I realized dark lines slotted the sunlight, and I squinted, trying to figure out what I was seeing. The lines across the light turned out to be the bars of a gate, something to keep nosy people from exploring, I assumed. On the other side, green countryside dappled in the sun's rays spread out before us. It was an almost tranquil view, and felt like a huge contrast to what we'd just experienced.

I reached the bars and banged my palms against them. They rattled under my hands, but didn't budge. A padlock held the gate locked to an iron bolt embedded into the rock.

Kingsley's voice came from over my shoulder. "The key's on your left, on the wall. It should be on a hook, right there."

I looked around, trying to spot the key, though this part of the wall was still in darkness.

"On your left, Darcy." His tone was a combination of frustration and amusement. "Not your right!"

Damn, I was normally good at that kind of thing. Everything that had happened had left me flustered.

Twisting in the correct direction, I spotted the key hanging from the hook in the rock. It was close enough that someone on the other side of the gate would have been able to reach it, but only if they knew it was there. A person would never have found it accidentally—just like the movable wall I'd slept next to night after night.

My fingers shook as I unhooked the key. I fumbled and dropped it to the ground with a clink, and stooped to pick the key up again. I hoped I'd be able to get it in the lock without doing something stupid and flicking it out of reach or something. There wasn't enough space for Kingsley to get past me and do it himself, so I had to get my unruly digits under control.

"How's Lorcan doing?" I asked, trying to think about something other than myself and the possibility I might end up getting us all trapped in here. If the men who'd been shooting at us in the house followed us down the tunnel, and I wasn't able to get the gate open, they'd shoot us like fish in a barrel.

Alex's voice sounded from farther down the tunnel. "He's okay. Just get us out of here."

"I'm trying!"

I managed to get the key in the lock, turned it, and the gate swung open. There was no sign of rust or creakiness. Someone had kept the exit clear and in working order for a reason. They'd predicted something like this might happen.

We stumbled out into the sunlight, me leading the way, my eyes streaming from the bright light as I squinted against it. Kingsley followed, and then we both turned to help Alex and Lorcan stand up out of the tunnel. Lorcan looked dangerously pale, his tattoos contrasting with the white of his skin. His dark eyes appeared sunken, as though he'd aged ten years in the last half an hour. But he was still conscious, and moving around, and so I took that as a good sign.

With the three men out of the way, I ducked down and peered back into the tunnel. My ears strained as I listened for movement—either from the men attacking us having followed us, or more hopefully, Clay and Isaac.

"No one is coming, Darcy," called Alex. "I pulled the wall hiding the tunnel shut behind us. We have to go."

I turned my attention from the tunnel. I didn't want to feel like I was running, but I had to think about Lorcan, too. Delaying us would only make things more dangerous for him. He needed help as quickly as possible.

Straightening, I took in the new surroundings. Back in the direction we'd come was the house, but it was some distance away now. In the opposite direction was a rougher terrain of trees which thickened into woodland. As though they already knew exactly where they were going, the men started to run in toward the trees. Alex still had his arm around Lorcan's waist so they moved as one. Kingsley paused and glanced back at me then gestured for me to get a move on.

I ran to catch up with him. "What about the others?" I managed between panted breaths. "Where are they?"

The running didn't appear to be affecting Kingsley in the slightest. "They'll be coming. They had something to do first."

"What?"

He didn't answer me. Was he just trying to cover up the possibility that Clay and Isaac might already be dead? I suddenly spotted what we were running toward. It wasn't the cover of the woodland. An SUV was parked between the tree trunks—clearly intended to be our escape vehicle. I should have been relieved to see it, but instead my jaw tightened and my lower lip quivered. I blinked back tears at the thought of leaving without the others. Would they think we'd just abandoned them?

The boom of a huge explosion smacked sound and light into the air. Even from this distance, the blast of heat struck me from behind, pitching me forward. The sky was filled with pieces of flying debris, smoke, and ash. An eerie silence settled around us, even the birds in the nearby trees stunned into momentary silence.

Kingsley reached down and helped me back to my feet. I dared to look back. Where the house had stood there was now only a burning pile of concrete, brick and timber. Smoke billowed into the air, thick and black, the scent of it carried on a light breeze toward us. Red and orange flames licked across the remaining structure. I let out a cry of horror and clamped my hand over my mouth. *Oh, God!* Were Clay and Isaac still in the house? There was no way they could have survived that.

None of the men said anything, but continued the way we were headed. Kingsley tried to help me along, but I pulled back on him.

"Wait, stop! We have to go back."

He shook his head, his expression grim. "No time. They'll be here any minute."

I knew who he was talking about when he said 'they.' The men with the guns. Though it tore me apart to think Clay and Isaac might be trapped inside the burning house, I knew there was nothing I could do to save them. Trying would mean sacrificing our lives, and there was no point in the others dying, too.

We reached the SUV. Kingsley yanked open the unlocked door and jumped in behind the wheel. Alex helped Lorcan into the back seat, while I climbed in the passenger side. I gasped for breath, but I didn't think it was from the running, but more the sheer terror and dismay at what had happened. My hands trembled in my lap, and I couldn't seem to think straight.

Beside me, Kingsley pulled down the visor, and the keys dropped out into his hand. He plunged them into the ignition, and the engine roared to life. He jammed his foot on the accelerator and pulled out from under the trees, dust bursting up from behind the wheels.

I dared to look back at the burning mass of the house. From beside the smoldering building, a dot emerged, growing bigger by the moment. A second car.

"Someone's coming," I cried. "It could be Isaac and Clay!"

Kingsley glanced over at me, his expression tight. "It's not Isaac and Clay."

I understood what that meant. If it wasn't them, it was the men who'd attacked the house.

Alex wound down the back window, stuck the rifle out of the gap. He fired off a couple of shots, the sound impossibly loud in the confines of the vehicle. The car got closer. I still had the gun in my hand. I could help. Kingsley was driving and Lorcan was out of action. This was an emergency.

Not bothering to ask permission, I wound down my window and leaned out.

"Get back in, Darcy!" Kingsley yelled.

"No!"

The vehicle was getting closer now. We bumped and jolted over the uneven terrain, but I held the gun in a firing-ready position, my arms straight, leaning as far out of the window as I dared, trying to balance between getting a good shot and making a target of myself.

I aimed the gun, aligning the front sight with the rear sight, just as my dad had taught me. I focused on my target, and my heart stopped. I'd spotted who was in the passenger seat of the car. Hollan.

Rage burst inside me, and I took a deep breath and held it, then pulled the trigger. A bullet cracked through the windshield of the other car, but I didn't think I'd hit the son of a bitch. He was responsible for the deaths of Clay and Isaac as well as my father. No man had ever deserved to die more.

I pulled the trigger again, and fired off another couple of shots, but my emotions had gotten the better of me, and they missed their mark.

In the back seat, Alex also fired. His aim was better, and he shot out the front tire of the vehicle behind us, sending it skidding off to the right. Kingsley put his foot down, increasing the distance between us. I wanted to tell him to stop and go back, so we could put a bullet in Hollan's head and end him once and for all, but a number of other dark spots were racing toward us from the burning house. More vehicles were coming after us.

A new vehicle burst out of the tree line, racing alongside us. I screamed, expecting to receive more gunfire at any moment, but then I spotted two familiar faces. Clay was driving, Isaac in the passenger seat. My eyes filled with tears of relief, and I gave a small cry. They were okay.

We bumped off the rough terrain and onto a small track. Kingsley put his foot down, the change in road allowing him to accelerate even further and put more space between us and the approaching vehicles.

Eventually, we lost sight of Hollan and his men, and we drove away, leaving the house burning behind us.

Chapter Twenty-five

In the back of the car, Alex worked on Lorcan. He tore off his shirt, leaving Lorcan bare-chested. The bullet wound was in Lorcan's shoulder, but looked as though it had penetrated the bulk of his muscle rather than bone. There didn't appear to be too much fresh bleeding, but dried blood that appeared almost black smeared across his numerous tattoos. The sight of it made my heart stumble in my chest.

"There's a bottle of water and a first aid kit in the glove box," said Alex. "Grab it for me."

I did as I was asked, quickly retrieving both items and handing them back to Alex. Alex got to work cleaning up the wound using some cotton wool and the water, then hunted in the first aid box. "The bullet's still lodged in there. I'm going to need to get it out. This is going to hurt, okay?"

Lorcan hadn't said a word, but I saw him grit his teeth and nod.

Alex swabbed down the area with an antiseptic wipe. "I could do with iodine, but this is the best we have in the circumstances."

"Just get on with it," Lorcan growled.

Alex had found the tweezers. I watched Lorcan's face, and then reached between the seats to grab his hand. He glanced up at me as my fingers laced with his. "I'll break your fingers, princess."

I gave him a grim smile and squeezed his hand in reassurance. "I can handle it."

Alex got to work, easing the tweezers into the wound to remove the bullet. Fresh blood dribbled from the bullet hole, down Lorcan's bare arm, and the sight of the metal digging into his shoulder made my stomach turn, but I didn't look away. Lorcan gave a strange keening sound in the back his throat, but his eyes locked onto mine and his fingers held on tight. I held his gaze, wishing I could take some of the pain away, trying to give him strength through eye contact alone, however inadequate it felt.

"Got it." Alex pulled away and held out the tweezers to display the bullet gripped in its metal tips.

Lorcan took his hand from mine and held it out to Alex. Alex dropped the bullet into his palm.

"I'll add it to the collection," Lorcan growled. He still looked in pain, but some of the color was returning to his face.

Alex used some Steri-Strips to hold the wound together, and then covered it up with a patch of gauze. "There you go, good as new."

I sat back in my seat, thankful Lorcan was going to be okay, and that Clay and Isaac were safe in the car following us.

"Where are we going?" I asked Kingsley, glancing over at him as he drove.

"To a safe house. It's only another hour or so."

We rode in silence, the vehicle containing Clay and Isaac following close behind. Despite being comparatively safe, tension ran high. There was a chance we'd be hijacked at any moment, and I found myself constantly checking behind to see if any strange vehicles followed. The road was quiet, but that didn't stop each of us tensing every time another car drove by.

Finally, we slowed, and Kingsley took a couple of smaller tracks, away from the main road and into what felt like the middle of nowhere. The asphalt ran out, and we bumped and jolted down the uneven terrain. I glanced around, trying to spot a sign to give me an idea of where this new place was, but there was nothing. It felt as though we were heading down an abandoned loggers' trail, taking us right in the depths of the forest.

The trees cleared, revealing a single story log cabin. Kingsley pulled up in front of the property, and the second vehicle parked up beside us.

Kingsley killed the engine. "Here we are."

The safe house was a contrast to the big, luxurious house we'd been in before. Not that it mattered, though I worried the whole time that Hollan's men were going to find us.

I climbed out of the car at the same time Clay did. How I'd felt when I thought he'd been killed still remained fresh in my mind and heart, and I ran straight to him, throwing my arms around his neck and hugging him tight. He responded by looping his arms around my waist and pulling me hard against him.

"I thought you and Isaac were dead," I said against his neck, his hair tickling my nose.

He pulled away and grinned. "Nah, it takes a lot more than armed men and an exploding house to kill us, sugar."

I glanced over to find Isaac still watching me, his arms folded. I offered him a consolatory smile. "I'm glad you're okay, too."

His lips twisted, and he didn't respond, causing something inside my chest to tighten.

Alex helped Lorcan out of the vehicle, but Lorcan already seemed stronger. His left hand clutched at his right shoulder, and he was able to move without needing further assistance. Together we all headed toward the cabin, and Kingsley did the honors of opening the door. The inside was basic but comfortable—a couple of couches, a kitchen at the rear, a few doors which led off to what I assumed were bedrooms and a bathroom. It was nothing like the house we'd left burning to the ground, but we were all still alive and back together again.

"What happened back there?" I asked, looking to Clay. "Who set the explosion?"

"We did," said Isaac. "We were compromised. It's part of our escape plan."

Kingsley shook his head, his brow drawn down, lips pinched. "How did they find out where the house was? We've been there for years and never been compromised."

Isaac turned to me, his stare cold and hard, and my stomach twisted. "What were you really doing last night, Darcy? You didn't go downstairs to get a glass of water, did you?"

There was no point in lying. My eyes filled with tears, but I swiped them away, angry at myself. I had done this. I had gotten Lorcan shot. It was my fault for being a thoughtless idiot. "I'm sorry. I called my Aunt Sarah. I just wanted to let her know I was safe."

"You called her? From the house phone?"

I nodded, feeling myself shrink in his icy gaze. He was furious with me, and I didn't blame him. He had every right to be, and so did the others. They should have kept me down in the cellar. Everyone would have been safer that way. I hated myself for what I'd done.

"I'm sorry," I pleaded again. "I knew she'd be worried—"

"Did it ever occur to you that Hollan might have been there? He most likely had the phones tapped, waiting for you to call. He was probably sitting beside your aunt as you spoke to her."

My eyes widened. "No! She would have said something if he'd been there. She would have told me."

"Not if she'd been told not to. If he made out like you'd been kidnapped, they wouldn't have wanted you alerting the kidnapper to the presence of the FBI."

I remembered how it had taken a little while for Aunt Sarah to answer the phone, and I'd assumed she'd been sleeping, but then she'd sounded sharp and wide awake. My hand went to my mouth in horror. Had Hollan been sitting beside her the whole time? The delay in her answering the phone had been them turning on the tracing equipment. They'd been waiting for me to call the whole time.

"No," I said, shaking my head, but more in dismay at my own actions than denying what he said was true. "No—"

To my shock and surprise, Isaac grabbed me by both arms. "For fuck's sake, Darcy! What the hell did you think you were playing at? Do you think this is some kind of game? We gave you an opportunity for you to show us you could be trusted, and instead you almost got us all killed!"

Tears streamed down my face. "I'm sorry. I wasn't thinking!"

He gave me a small shake. "We should never have let you out of the cellar. Lorcan could be dead right now because of you."

"I know. I'm sorry," I repeated, not knowing what else to say. There was nothing I could say to make this better. I had messed up, big time. I didn't blame them if they never trusted me again.

His face was up close to mine, his body pinning me. I saw anger in the green depths of his eyes, but also something else, something that sent my heart racing for all the wrong reasons. "Why do you always insist on acting like such a little brat?"

I wanted to tell him I was sorry again, but what would be the point? I'd said it as many times as I could, and now it was falling on deaf ears. I needed to show them they could trust me. Actions were more important now.

"This isn't all her fault," Clay said from close behind Isaac's shoulder.

Isaac released me and turned away to point a finger at him. "Stop sticking up for her. Just because you stuck your tongue down her throat, doesn't mean she's in the right."

My face flamed with fire, and I exchanged a glance with Clay.

Isaac looked back to me, but something in his eyes had changed, a spark of an idea dancing in his gaze. "And you need to remember that the five of us work as a team. What one of us is involved with, the rest of us get to be, too."

What did that mean?

He cocked a finger at me. "Come here."

Meek and compliant, tears drying in salty tracks down my face, I took the couple of steps needed to close the distance he'd only just put between us. He was right. I'd messed up big time. I could have gotten one of us killed, or worse.

"We work together now, do you understand? No more creeping around. You put us in danger, and you put yourself in danger. Everything we'd done since this whole thing started has been to try to keep you safe. I wish you would understand that."

I nodded. "I do."

I didn't want to come between the guys. I wanted to bring them back together.

Isaac was so close to me, I could smell smoke and danger, and everything that shouldn't excite me, but did. My heart fluttered like butterfly wings, my breath catching.

"Why can't you see that everything we've done has been to protect you, Darcy?" he growled.

I was aware of the others all watching. Other than Clay, none of them made a move to defend me, but why should they? I was the one who'd done them wrong. I deserved whatever punishment Isaac planned on delivering to me.

He trapped my chin between his powerful fingers, tilting my face to his. My breath caught. The fury was gone from his eyes now, and replaced by something needier. They'd all done their part in taking me, and on some deep level I knew I belonged to them all.

I thought he was going to kiss me, but he didn't. With a jerk of his chin over his shoulder, he beckoned Clay over.

Clay moved quickly, a few steps of his usual swagger, and he was behind me. His strong body pressed up against my back, and his arms looped under mine to wrap around my waist. I was trapped between them, with Isaac holding my chin and Clay supporting me from behind. My pulse quickened in anticipation of what was about to happen. Maybe I should be afraid, but I wasn't. No, I was excited.

Isaac stared into my eyes, capturing me in his intense gaze. While one hand had hold of my chin, the other slipped down the front of my body. I still wore Alex's oversized t-shirt, and my ancient jeans which had definitely seen better days. There was nothing sexy about me in that moment, and yet fire burned inside me at Isaac's touch.

We could have died, Lorcan was hurt, I looked like shit, but none of that mattered. It was crazed and wild, and I'd never done anything like this before in my life, but I allowed Isaac to push his hand down the front of my jeans.

From behind, Clay took my weight, holding me up. A hardness pushed against the small of my back, and I knew this was exciting Clay as much as it was me.

My breath hitched as Isaac's fingers moved lower, his fingers slipping beneath my panties, and through the small patch of curls at the juncture of my thighs. His other hand remained steadying my chin, forcing my eyes to remain on his as he delved deeper.

I let out a whimper.

He parted my most secret folds, and his finger slipped inside me. My knees buckled, but Clay held me up from behind. The heat of his skin burned against my neck, and his breathing became ragged as my own arousal began to build. My wetness made Isaac's passage easy, and he moved his finger deeper inside me, the base of his hand pressing against my most sensitive spot, giving me something to grind against. I was aware of the others in the room, of heated breaths and mounting tension.

A familiar pressure built at my core, tightening and spreading. My breath grew shallow, and small moans crept unbidden from my throat. I wanted to reach out to Isaac, to touch him, to hold him, but somehow I knew that wasn't what he wanted. He wasn't doing this for me and him. This was for all of us, to bind us as a group. To make me understand that I belonged to each of them now, and watching me orgasm somehow connected us all.

As I ground down on Isaac's hand, Clay's hands moved up, cupping my breasts over the top of the t-shirt I wore. His thumbs and forefingers found the already sensitized buds of my nipples and he pinched both, hard. The material protected the tightened peaks, but it hurt enough to make me buck between the two men, letting out a cry of surprise and a hint of pain.

A second finger pushed inside me, stretching me. I was a shaking, shuddering mess, a film of sweat springing up on my forehead, chest, and upper lip. Unable to look into Isaac's intense eyes any longer, or to acknowledge the three other men still watching, I squeezed my eyes shut, focusing inward. Isaac must have sensed how close I was, as his fingers curled inward, searching for the little pad of flesh on my inside wall that would propel me to the next level. My fists clenched and unclenched, wanting to grab Isaac's biceps and connect myself to him in some way, but though he said this was to bring us all together, even with his fingers thrusting deep and hard inside me, I still sensed the distance between us. Instead, I held Clay's forearms as they remained wrapped around me, and knew I was digging my blunt nails into his skin as I slowly lost control.

I came hard and fast on Isaac's hand, leaving me gasping for breath, the little shock waves shuddering through me. I knew I'd have left his digits soaked, and a hot flush crept up from my chest, wrapping around my throat.

Isaac pulled his hand from my jeans and dropped his hold on my chin. Clay released me as well, and took a step back, putting space between us again.

"Do you do that to all the new recruits?" I said, my voice breathy, trying to use humor to cover my embarrassment.

The corner of Isaac's mouth twitched. "Only ones who won't accept what we are."

I barely dared to ask. "What are you?"

"We're a team, Darcy, and you're a part of that now. We all want the same thing, we're all working toward the same goal. Your defenses were so high I could barely see over them. I needed to break them down so you'd let us in."

I figured Isaac's defenses were at least as high as mine, but I managed to hold back the retort.

But he was right, and guilt tickled its uneasy fingers at my insides. I'd gone against them and done something they'd specifically told me not to do, and look where that had gotten us, but that wasn't all. I'd been holding the most important thing of all from them, and now I realized everything I'd done had been wrong.

Clay stepped forward so I could see him, his head tilted to one side slightly, his hair hanging over his face. "What are you thinking, sugar?"

I could feel them all watching me. Were they all thinking about sex right now, about how I could smell myself on the air? About what Isaac had just done? Or were they straight back to business?

"You can trust us, Darcy," Alex said.

Kingsley nodded. "He's right. You can trust us."

I looked between all their faces, even Lorcan, who'd remained seated on the couch, still looking pained, but engaged in the conversation. I caught his eye, and he gave me a small nod to show me he agreed.

"I'm thinking that I haven't been completely honest with you."

They exchanged glances.

Isaac's green eyes narrowed. "About what?"

"When Kingsley hypnotized me yesterday and I said I couldn't remember, I lied."

Isaac frowned, and his expression was mirrored by the others. "What do you mean?"

"I did remember what my father said."

"You remembered the numbers?"

These men had done so much for me, even though I hadn't liked or appreciated it at first. They'd saved me from Hollan and his men when they'd first come to my house, and though they'd treated me roughly, my insistence at fighting them every step of the way hadn't left them with much choice.

And with my heart-beating hard, I told them the code.

THE END

LIKE WHAT YOU'VE READ? Book two, Unraveling Darkness, will be released November 27th 2017!

Acknowledgments

Hacking Darkness was a dip into a new genre for me—that of Reverse Harem. I've often written books where I've had to choose between the guys for the main character, and it's been so refreshing knowing Darcy hasn't had to do that in this story. I'm almost finished writing the first draft of book two, and I've loved moving her relationship forward with the guys—some more than others.

As always with a book, I couldn't have done this on my own! Huge thanks to my first reader and fellow author, Lily Harlem, who gave me tons of great suggestions for the story. Thanks as always to my long time editor, Lori Whitwam, whose hard work always makes a huge difference to mine. I wouldn't be able to do it without you! Thank you to my proofreaders on this book, Tammy Payne and Karey McComish, for catching those pesky typos!

Many thanks to Daqri from Covers by Combs for creating the fabulous cover for Hacking Darkness. You created exactly what I had in my head, and I love it! Can't wait to see what the next books in the series turn out like.

And finally, thanks to everyone over at RH readers—both the readers and authors alike. I peppered you all with questions during the writing of this book, and everyone was so helpful, no matter what I asked, and I'm hugely grateful!

Finally, thank you to you, the reader, for sticking with me on this journey.

Thanks for reading!

Marissa. XXX

About the Author

Marissa Farrar has always been in love with being in love. But since she's been married for numerous years and has three young daughters, she's conducted her love affairs with multiple gorgeous men of the fictional persuasion.

The author of thirty novels, she has been a full time author for the last six years. She predominantly writes paranormal romance and urban fantasy, but has branched into contemporary fiction as well.

If you want to know more about Marissa, then please visit her website at www.marissa-farrar.blogspot.com. You can also find her at her facebook page, www.facebook.com/marissa.farrar.author or follow her on twitter @marissafarrar.

She loves to hear from readers and can be emailed at marissafarrar@hotmail.co.uk and to stay updated on all her new Reverse Harem books, just sign up to her newsletter! https://landing.mailerlite.com/webforms/landing/e2x3e1

Also by the Author

The Monster Trilogy:
Defaced
Denied
Delivered

The Mercenary Series:
Skewed
Warped
Flawed
Judged

The Spirit Shifters Series:
Autumn's Blood
Saving Autumn
Autumn Rising
Autumn's War
Avenging Autumn
Autumn's End

The Serenity Series:
Alone
Buried

Captured
Dominion
Endless

The Dhampyre Chronicles:
Twisted Dreams
Twisted Magic

The Flux Series
Flux
After Flux

The Blood Courtesans Vampire Romance:
Stolen

Contemporary Fiction Novels
The Second Chances
Dirty Shots
Cut Too Deep
Survivor
The Sound of Crickets

Dark Fantasy/horror novels:
Underlife
The Dark Road

Made in the USA
Middletown, DE
27 June 2020